THE ENDS OF THE EARTH

Bethany Campbell

Harlequin Books

TORONTO • NEW YORK • LONDON
AMSTERDAM • PARIS • SYDNEY • HAMBURG
STOCKHOLM • ATHENS • TOKYO • MILAN

ISBN 0-373-03079-7

Harlequin Romance first edition October 1990

This story, its setting and characters are entirely fictional but were inspired by actual events.
My sincere thanks to the generous people in Barrow, Anchorage and Seattle who shared their knowledge and experiences with me. What rings true in this book is theirs. The mistakes are mine alone. It is dedicated to those who worked so long and so gallantly on the ice.

Printed in U.S.A.

‘‘Northern Lights,’’ he muttered

Tonight the lights had come up with unusual suddenness—as if they had been lying in wait for the appearance of this woman.

She looked enchanted, intoxicated. Her wonder was so intense it somehow embarrassed him—went counter to his theories about her and the Martinson family in general. Hal took refuge in what he knew best—facts. ‘‘Charged particles from the sun bombard the oxygen and nitrogen in the upper atmosphere—’’

She interrupted with the most unscientific thing possible, her face shining like a kid’s. ‘‘It’s magic.’’

Her observation disturbed him. Her face had the rapt expression of a woman in love. She looked radiant enough to wrench a man’s heart out of his chest. No wonder Keenan hadn’t dared face her.

I want this woman out of here, he thought darkly. *As soon as possible*.

Bethany Campbell, an English major and textbook consultant, calls her writing world her "hidey-hole," that marvelous place where true love always wins out. Her hobbies include writing poetry and thinking about that little scar on Harrison Ford's chin. She laughingly admits that her husband, who produces videos and writes comedy, approves of the first one only.

Books by Bethany Campbell

HARLEQUIN ROMANCE

2726—AFTER THE STARS FALL
2779—ONLY A WOMAN
2803—A THOUSAND ROSES
2815—SEA PROMISES
2852—THE LONG WAY HOME
2877—HEARTLAND
2911—FLIRTATION RIVER
2949—THE DIAMOND TRAP
3000—THE LOST MOON FLOWER
3019—THE SNOW GARDEN
3045—THE HEART OF THE SUN
3062—DANCING SKY

HARLEQUIN INTRIGUE

65—PROS AND CONS
116—THE ROSE OF CONSTANT

CHAPTER ONE

"YOU DON'T WANT me to go to Alaska to write a story. What you want is for me to bring Keenan home. That's impossible. He went up there to get away from me. Thanks to you, he thinks I want to marry him. I mean, I *do* love him. But like a—a cousin or an uncle or something."

Jennifer shook her head in frustration. She was a tall young woman, just under six feet, with blond hair that she wore pulled back in one long braid.

Her grandfather, Dagobert Martinson, sat at his desk. At seventy-two, he was still lean and powerful, his white hair still thick, his blue eyes still quick and sharp. Behind him, his office window framed a view of the Golden Gate Bridge over a slightly misty bay.

Before him, resting on his desk, was a hollow crystal globe filled with shiny black liquid. The liquid was oil from Dagobert Martinson's first gusher, which had gushed him to wealth almost fifty years ago. Jen had always thought it a shame to fill such a beautiful globe with crude oil. From the time she was a child she had called it "the gunk ball."

For years her grandfather had liked her irreverence because it reminded him of his own. Much, however, had changed recently. He was no longer amused by any show of independent thought.

Jen crossed her legs and sat calmly, staring back at him with eyes just as blue and as stubborn as his. "I won't try to bring him back. The situation's impossible. You and Ferd have meddled with us too much. No more."

Silence ticked by as her grandfather's fuse burned down. *Three, two, one,* Jen counted to herself. *Zero.*

Dagobert Martinson's temper exploded on schedule. He slammed his blotter with his open hand. His desk calendar hopped as if in fright, and the oil in the crystal ball swayed ominously.

"First, don't ever say *impossible* to me. I've taken oil from beneath the sea. I've put satellites into space. I helped put a man in the White House. *Impossible* is not a word I recognize."

Jen knew better than to speak yet. Next, she thought with philosophical detachment, he's going to ask why I'm not wearing makeup. Then he'll yell about my clothes. Then he'll go into why I should be married.

Her grandfather pointed a gnarled and accusing finger at her. "Why don't you ever wear makeup? You could be a beautiful girl. Do you always have to look like you just climbed off a surfboard?"

Jen shrugged politely, as if the matter puzzled her as well. Nature had given her coloring that was dramatic enough for her tastes: she was deeply tanned, her blond hair streaked with platinum; a healthy flush colored her cheekbones; her eyes were blue, her lashes dark, her lips pink. When she put on makeup, it was like donning a false face.

"Another thing," fumed Dagobert, rising from his leather chair and starting to pace. "Those clothes. Today you look like you just came out of the jungle to sell your mangoes in the marketplace. What kind of outfit is that supposed to be? Whatever happened to lace and stuff?"

Jen glanced down mildly at her long batik skirt and matching blouse. They were fashionable and, although casual, expensive. She liked her clothes comfortable and individualistic. Lately her grandfather had taken it into his head that she should wear ruffles and flounces. She was too tall for frills, and she refused.

Dagobert stalked a few last paces and planted himself in front of his seated granddaughter. He glared down. "What's more, you ought to be married. It's time to make a home. Have babies."

Give a poor lonely old man some grandchildren, by Jiminy, Jen added mentally, watching his white eyebrows work up and down.

"Give a poor lonely old man some grandchildren, by Jiminy. It's time you settled down. You've played long enough. Too long, in fact."

Jen remained unperturbed. "I'm only twenty-three. I want a career. I want to do something with my life. I want to see the world."

"Bah!" Her grandfather turned his back on her and stared out the window. "You've got San Francisco. Who needs the world? You should be having a family. You don't need any more career than that."

She looked at his straight back. Its rigidity seemed to accuse her of terrible crimes. She loved her grandfather a great deal, and she knew precisely why he was acting this way. But even though she understood him, her patience was starting to fail. "You didn't used to say that. You used to tell me I could be anything I wanted. I want to be a reporter."

"I used to tell you a lot of foolishness." He kept his back to her. "I was too easy on you because—well, because. You're playing at reporting, that's all. Do you think you actually have a talent for that sort of thing?''

She took a breath so sharply it hurt. Her grandfather played rough and often he played unfairly. A year and a half ago she seldom saw this side of him. Lately she saw it all the time.

''It's a little early to know if I have talent. I've only been out of college a year.''

''Where you were a thoroughly ordinary student. All you cared about was skiing. And surfing. Never had to face a responsibility in your life.'' He turned and stared at her coolly. ''Admit it—you wouldn't have a decent job today without Ferd Brubecker and me.''

When she was silent, he smiled. ''Afraid to admit it?''

The air between them crackled. He was almost right, she thought, shifting uncomfortably. Her grades in college had been adequate but hardly impressive. She'd worked hard on the student newspaper but not nearly hard enough in the classroom.

Those carefree days now seemed centuries ago. She'd lived for three things then: to write funny little stories for the college paper, to surf in the summer and to ski in the winter. She'd been a California golden girl, intent on having fun. She'd given little thought to tomorrows.

Then the world came apart. Three days before she was to graduate, her brothers, Harry and Dwayne, were killed. Dwayne had been twenty-eight years old, engaged to the daughter of Dagobert's best friend, Ferd Brubecker. Harry had been twenty-five.

They had been in the family plane, flying to Galveston. Jen had kissed them both goodbye after breakfast. She had laughed and said, ''Don't fall out of the sky.''

Two hours later, both were dead. Jen didn't attend her own graduation. She was at a double funeral, holding

Dagobert's arm, wondering how either of them would survive.

Numbed, not thinking clearly, she'd taken the first job offer that came her way, unmindful that it came from Dagobert's closest friend, Ferd Brubecker. Dazed by her brothers' deaths, she'd wanted to lose herself in work, to work so hard she couldn't think of anything else.

Her grandfather had always been the center of her life, but he changed after the boys died. Before, he had indulged her and encouraged her to run free. Now he was pulling in hard on her reins, trying to arrange her life.

He had always expected Harry and Dwayne to carry on his name and work. He had raised them to be disciplined young men, cautious of change, careful to listen, quick to obey. If the old man spoiled Jen, made her as hardheaded and independent as himself, it didn't matter. She was a girl. He had cherished her, spoiled her and rejoiced that she had a spirit as free as his own.

He had forged the boys into good corporate soldiers, molded them to take over the rule of the Martinson Corporation. As for Jen, Dagobert had decreed, let her go her own way and above all else enjoy herself. What difference did it make?

Then the plane had crashed. For a time it seemed to Jen that her grandfather's world had crashed with it and he would never be the same. But Dagobert had lived through much.

He had survived the untimely death of his wife, and later the loss of his only son, Jen's father. Her father and mother had been driving to Tahoe to celebrate a second honeymoon when their car was struck by a truck that veered out of control, killing them instantly. Jen, hardly a year old at the time, could not remember them at all. Dagobert had grieved deeply but he went on. He raised the three grandchildren—only to see two of them die in a way just as unnecessary, just as meaningless as his son and daughter-in-law had.

He survived this latest loss in part by changing his desires and plans. He could no longer emotionally afford Jen to be his pet, his indulgence. She must somehow replace Harry and Dwayne, the men. She would do it by having sons of her own, bringing forth new male heirs to rule Dagobert's kingdom. She was his sole hope. His sole hope, however, had ideas of her own.

Unfortunately Dagobert had created Jennifer to think for herself, to go her own way, to be different and to dare. Now, he had to recreate her. Foolishly he had given her the cool confidence to look him in the eye and defy him. Now he must beat her down and bend her to his will. If he had endowed her too generously with courage, now he would steal it back. He had to.

"You've played a year at this job. It's long enough." He smiled in his old beguiling way. "Now it's time to take on some real responsibility. Make everybody happy. Marry Keenan."

Jen sighed, tired of hearing about it. Keenan was Ferd Brubecker's only grandson. Ferd and Dagobert had gone through four years of the Second World War together. They had survived prison camp in the Pacific together and were literally closer than brothers.

Back home each man had used his prodigious will to amass a fortune. Ferd Brubecker's empire was in publishing; he owned newspapers all over the country, including many along the Pacific coast.

Like two princes of old, Dagobert and Fred had dreamed of uniting their wealth into one mighty kingdom. Obliging as usual, Dwayne had fallen in love with one of Ferd's granddaughters, Clare. Now both old men had decided that if Clare couldn't marry Dwayne, the only fitting alternative was that Jen marry Ferd's grandson, Keenan. It was an idiotic idea, Jen thought, one right out of the middle ages, and neither she nor Keenan wanted it.

Keenan was sweet, shy and self-conscious, and Jen had known him all her life. He had been especially kind when she was grieving for her brothers. But then, with shock, he had recognized the matchmaking gleam in the eyes of their grandfathers.

Keenan, who had plans and a career of his own, panicked when he realized the plot. He must have fretted that he had gotten too deeply involved with Jen and feared she looked on him as more than a friend. He had fled and hidden himself at the ends of the earth. When Jen realized what had happened, she tried to write to him, explaining. For eight months, he had returned her letters unopened and not sent her so much as a postcard. She could find no way to convince him that she didn't wish him sacrificed upon the altar of matrimony. As fond as she was of Keenan, she was frustrated by his romantic paranoia.

She had depended on him too much after the boys' deaths, she supposed. She had turned to him the way she had always turned to Dwayne, her elder brother. She hadn't meant for Keenan to misunderstand, but lately all her relationships seemed doomed to twist monstrously out of shape.

"Ferd says you don't show any real enthusiasm for reporting," her grandfather said. "Not really."

"Ferd gave me a job—" Jen tossed her head so the long gold braid swung "—but he's never given me a chance. There's a difference."

"You have a chance now," Dagobert wheedled. "Your editor wants you to go to Alaska. Do a real feature story. What's the matter? Scared to take the chance?"

"I don't *want* to take it," Jen shot back. "This trip isn't my editor's idea. You and Ferd cooked this up. I know you two. And I know what you're trying to do."

"What are we trying to do?" Dagobert tried to feign innocence. He was no good at it.

"First," Jen accused, "you got Ferd to offer me a job when I wasn't thinking clearly. I just took it to be near you both. You both knew I wouldn't like it. I don't want to be a society reporter. I'm not the society type."

"You wanted in journalism." He smiled like a crocodile. "Oh, how I've spoiled you. Lots of women would kill for your job."

"Phooey," Jen said with the blunt inelegance she'd inherited directly from Dagobert. "All I ever write is wedding stories. I've probably written 'The bride wore white' a million times. It's boring."

"You want a change of pace? Then stop being contrary. Go to Alaska."

"To do a story on Keenan? No. I told my editor I won't, I told Ferd, and now I'm telling you." Jen crossed her arms and stared at him unhappily. She missed the man Dagobert used to be, the one she had grown up loving and teasing. That man would never have bullied her so mercilessly or tried so maddeningly to force his will upon her.

He picked up a gold letter opener. He opened his drawer and withdrew an enormous russet apple. "Defy your editor and he'll fire you. It won't be Brubecker's fault or mine. He'll have no choice."

He began to peel away the apple's skin. "Do you know what happens if you're fired?" he asked. "Here. Have some apple. It's sweet." He sliced off a section and held it toward her.

She refused it. "I know what happens, all right. I never work on a major paper again. You and Ferd will see to that. You've already seen to it. I've tried to find another job. I can't. You old fox."

He ate the apple slice himself. "Ah, juicy and delicious. Yes. You'll never work again. At least on any decent paper. Oh, you might go out to the badlands or the swamp or some extremely small town, far from the beach and the mountains—and we both know how you'd hate that...."

She set her jaw. "Dagobert, you don't understand. I don't love Keenan."

"Pah!" Dagobert's voice vibrated with disgust. "What do you know? You're only a child. Of course you love him. He's your own kind. You broke his heart and he left. He's up in Alaska waiting for you to grow up and realize your own feelings."

"I never broke his heart. He doesn't love me. Thanks to you, he's scared to death of me." Jen, usually slow to anger, felt it creeping through her. She knew Dagobert loved her, but he was being impossible, completely and utterly.

"You had a misunderstanding and broke his heart. He went off to lick his wounds." Dagobert peeled more skin from the apple.

"Keenan helped me when I needed help." Jen found herself clenching her fists for emphasis. "But I didn't break his heart. The only misunderstanding we ever had was that he thought I was serious about him. He didn't go off to Alaska just to get away from me. He went to get away from Ferd. And from you. Keenan wants a life of his own. Can't anybody understand that? Can't Ferd admit he's an overbearing old . . . poot? Why doesn't he pay some attention to his granddaughters? Marry them off. He has three."

Slowly, almost surgically, Dagobert began to remove another slice of the apple. "Three granddaughters. But only one grand*son*. All right. I admit it. Ferd's worried. He wants you to go to Alaska, talk to Keenan. Bring him back."

"That's impossible," Jen insisted for the third time. "Keenan's a grown man. He's doing what he wants. If Ferd can't accept that—"

Dagobert slapped his desk so that the calendar hopped once more and the oil surged blackly in the crystal ball. "Ferd doesn't have to *accept* anything. Ferd creates situations that *other* people accept. And what you're going to accept is going to Alaska—to see Keenan. Write a story on him. And talk some sense into him.... Bring him home."

Jen could bear it no longer. Her grandfather was standing behind his desk, leaning his fists on it. She rose, went before him and she, too, leaned on the desk so that she could look him directly in the eye. She was nearly as tall as he, and her delicately rounded jaw had the same granite set as his long pointed one.

"There is, I repeat, no story on Keenan." She enunciated each word clearly, as if she were speaking to a stubborn child. "Keenan is somewhere in the arctic studying walrus. This may be big news in walrus circles, but not around here."

Her grandfather leaned across the desk, closer to her. "He's just been promoted. He's going to be assistant director of walrus research at the Arctic Research Facility."

"Bully for him. That's worth about a paragraph. I can write it from here."

"You're frightened." Dagobert's tone was sly. "You're afraid of your own emotions."

Jen's frayed patience snapped at last. A haze of anger descended on her, seemed to make the very air of the room dance. "I'm *not* frightened. You and Ferd want me to go to Alaska? Fine. I'll go to Alaska. You want me to talk to Keenan? Fine. I'll talk to Keenan. I'll tell him I'm not interested in him—he's safe from me. And maybe I'll even find a real feature story. A good one—and it won't be on Keenan."

Dagobert laughed. He shook his head. "You won't find any other story, Jen. You're not the type—can't you understand that? You haven't got that essential hunger for the news... or the ruthlessness. It's a hard business, news. It can be ugly. You were raised for finer things."

Her blue eyes flashed resentment. "Maybe I'll find a job up there where nobody'll try to run my life. Maybe I'll follow Keenan's example. Maybe I won't come back."

Her grandfather gave a derisive snort. Once more he was peeling the apple. "The important thing is that you're going. Good. Excellent."

Jen felt a pulse beating wildly in her temple. "Have you heard one word I've said?"

He nodded, as if bored. "Something about leaving California and finding work on an iceberg. You're not the type, Golden Girl. You were born to get a suntan, not goosebumps. If you stay up there, you'll be begging me to rescue you in a month. Probably less. I know my girl. Indeed, I do."

Jen's head took on a defiant tilt. "I will never, ever, as long as I live ask you for another favor."

He studied his apple slice, virginal and white between his arthritic fingers. "Care to bet? You're spoiled. You need to know how the real world works. You'll be begging for favors before a month is up."

He raised his eyes to meet hers. He studied her coolly. "Let's make a little bargain," he said. "Ask me for just one favor, and if it's granted, then you'll come home. You'll do as I say and behave yourself. If you don't marry Keenan, you'll find yourself someone else—that I approve of. Is it a deal?"

She regarded him as if he were a wily old serpent trying to bargain for her soul. She folded her arms. She nodded with the finality of someone who will never back down. "Fine. I said I won't ask for favors. I meant it. If I do, then I'll live the life you want. But I warn you, Dagobert. You won't win."

"No? I don't lose, you know." He ate a last slice of apple and smacked his lips in satisfaction. "You'll be back. Don't worry. I know human nature."

He handed her the apple core. "Be a good girl and drop this in the outer office, will you? The way you used to when you were a little tyke? Ah, what happened to that sweet child?"

Reluctantly she took the apple core. It was cold, moist and ragged in her hand.

He opened his drawer and drew out a packet of tickets. "Here." His tone was dangerously pleasant. "Your plane tickets. Remember, Ferd is expecting you to talk to Keenan. You have an assignment. Don't accept the tickets unless you intend to do it. It wouldn't be honest."

She stretched out her hand and took the packet. For the first time her confidence wavered. She stood, twenty-three years old, her courage shaken, a set of tickets in one hand and the core of an apple in the other. The apple core made her feel as if she'd somehow accepted forbidden fruit, in spite of all her best efforts.

"I'll call Keenan," she said with false calm. "I'll tell him I'm coming."

Dagobert smiled. "Don't bother. He already knows. Ferd phoned."

She looked at him, startled. Had he known all along she'd be going? Had she played right into his hands?

Dagobert saw her moment of self-doubt. "Of course," he said smoothly, "the best and wisest thing would be if you and Keenan stopped all this nonsense and came home together. Took your rightful places in the family."

She gave him a stiff smile. "Goodbye," she said. "I may not be back. I mean it. And this may seem like a strange time to say it, but I will.... I love you."

She tossed the apple core in the air and caught it with a nonchalance she didn't feel. "So long, Dagobert," she said and gave another smile. It trembled slightly on her lips.

She turned and walked out of the office. Out of sheer bravado, she tossed the apple core again. She looked almost jaunty.

She got into the elevator and rode down numbly. A few moments later she found herself on the sidewalk, staring toward the bay with its veil of haze. The bright October sunshine hurt her eyes. She felt dazed, wounded and filled with conflicting emotions.

She was angry with her grandfather, yet she was sorry for him, too. It was almost as if her brothers' deaths had made him a bit insane. He was desperate to control events rather than let them control him, and there was something sad in his need to make her live out his dreams. She felt genuine pity for him. But also, for the first time in months, she felt strangely free.

She started down the street, barely noticing the people around her, or the green cable car clanging as it labored uphill. She had forgotten to toss the apple core away and still held it like some talisman for good or evil.

She was really doing it, she thought, both exhilarated and frightened. She was breaking away.

She would fly to Alaska. Ferd Brubecker owned no newspapers in Alaska; that she knew. There were cities in Alaska, big ones, and that meant papers, and papers meant a chance to work. She'd never again be naive enough to work for Ferd or take favors from him or her grandfather. Never.

Alaska seemed the perfect place for her. People always said you could leave the past behind when you went to Alaska, make a new life for yourself. She'd try.

She tossed the apple core up and caught it one last time. "Here goes nothing," she thought philosophically. She bit into the last remaining chunk of the fruit. It tasted like freedom. And as Dagobert had promised, it tasted sweet.

CHAPTER TWO

LOOK FOR A BIG BLONDE, Keenan Brubecker had told him. *She'll stand right out—a sun bunny lost in the snow. You can't miss her.*

Unfortunately, Hal Bailey thought, he'd already missed her. He'd meant to meet her plane, but a polar bear had lumbered onto the road, blocking his path for a good fifteen minutes.

The bear, a nice female, about a thousand pounds of her, had looked almost blue in the moonlight. She'd been a beautiful thing, gorgeous in the extreme, but he'd have to notify authorities that she was around and, in the meantime, she'd made him miss the blonde at the airport. Now he'd try the hotel. He opened its heavy door.

He pushed the furred hood of his parka back and stamped his feet. He was a fair-sized man, an inch or two over six feet tall, lanky but broad of shoulder. His skin was burnished by sun and wind, his hair was brown and his eyes were blue with the far-seeing, piercing gaze of someone who lives where the spaces stretch wide. His beard was a darker brown than his hair and touched here and there with the first traces of silver.

He was thirty-two years old, had the flat accent and the slow-tempoed speech of a native Middle-Westerner, and he prided himself on being a reasonable man. "When the world ends," Keenan Brubecker had once joked, "and everybody else is running in circles, look for the guy who's standing there taking notes on it. That'll be Hal."

Well, he thought, the world wasn't ending, but he had plenty on his hands. A research facility to run, a polar bear prowling the neighborhood, a pair of whales stuck in the ice, and now, when he least needed another complication, Brubecker's blonde, the granddaughter of that old plunderer, Dagobert Martinson.

Hal walked across the orange carpet of the hotel lobby. A pretty native girl, Inupiat Eskimo, sat behind the desk reading a magazine, smoking a cigarette and looking bored. Her hair was artificially curled, her lips and fingernails artificially red. Too bad, thought Hal, who liked things natural.

"Hello, Sonia," he said, putting his gloved fist on the desk. "I'm here for Brubecker's blonde. You got her?"

Sonia's boredom vanished when she recognized Hal Bailey. She smiled pertly, showing her dimples. "Why do you want Brubecker's blonde? Can't you find a girl of your own?"

Hal nodded gruffly to show he'd gotten the joke. "Yeah, yeah. Listen, she wasn't supposed to check in here. He got her a room at the facility. Tell me where to find her and then take her off your books, or whatever you do, will you?"

"She's in room 109," Sonia said. "Why's she staying at the facility? Helena's not going to like *that*."

"That'll be Helena and Brubecker's problem." Hal stripped off his gloves and glove liners. The town of Ultima was small—three thousand people. Brubecker was too smart to try to keep the blonde a secret, which was why everyone knew about her. Brubecker had more important secrets to keep. So far he had kept them. So far, so good, thought Hal.

"How are the whales?" Sonia asked, fluttering her eyelashes.

His answer was curt. "Still caught."

He started down the long hallway, unfastening his parka. He disliked the task he was about to start, but he'd given his promise to Brubecker, as a man and as a friend. More importantly, he'd given it to Helena, of whom he was protective. Helena had worked for him since he'd come to the arctic five years ago. She had been invaluable, irreplaceable. Nobody was going to ruin her happiness, not if Hal could help it.

He pounded unceremoniously on the door of room 109. He supposed he should have phoned from the lobby and announced himself, but it seemed a stupid waste of time.

What was this woman's first name, anyway, he thought testily. The bear blocking the road had knocked it smack out of his mind, where it had never been firmly wedged. The last name, Martinson, wasn't one he could forget. Old Dagobert Martinson was notorious for his disregard of the environment, and he owned a sizable chunk of MaLaBar, the company that had built the controversial Alaskan pipeline. It was rumored that at this very moment he was scheming to get his hooks into Bristol Bay.

Bristol Bay was one of Alaska's most fertile fish-breeding areas, and old Martinson had considerable political clout to call on if he wanted to get permission to drill there for more oil. As if that wasn't enough, now he'd sent his dizzy granddaughter up from California to pursue poor Brubecker.

He heard a hesitant scuffling sound inside, and the door opened a scant two inches, chained from within. He saw a wary blue eye, long-lashed and almost level with his own, looking out at him. Damn, he thought, what was her name? Why'd he ever let Brubecker talk him into this? Suddenly it all seemed like a terrible idea. He reminded himself it was more for Helena's sake than anything else.

"Yes?" she asked, her voice surprisingly firm.

He fumbled for a moment, then decided simply to get on with it. He groped in his pocket, took out his wallet and flashed his identity card. "I'm Dr. Hal Bailey from the Arctic Research Facility. I was supposed to meet you at the airport. Are you the Martinson woman? Brubecker's blonde?"

The blue eye blinked in surprise, and he saw ice form in its depths. "I'm *nobody's* blonde, cowboy. The name is Jennifer Martinson. *Ms* Martinson to you."

A cold one, thought Hal, one wanting special treatment. Well, she wouldn't get it from him. The woman was a nuisance, a menace to two of his favorite employees, and she stood for everything he despised, as well. The sooner she was gone, the better.

"Ms Martinson—" he said the name with a maximum of sarcasm "—I hope you haven't unpacked. Dr. Brubecker has a room for you at the facility. I'll take you there."

The blue eye narrowed suspiciously. "Why didn't he come himself?"

"He's over at the next village. There's a dead walrus. He wanted to look at its stomach contents."

Jen blinked hard. She believed the story because it seemed too ridiculous to be false. Besides, it sounded exactly like Keenan. He'd once invited her to go to Carmel to a seminar on chest ailments of the sea otter.

Unchaining the door, she swung it wide. She hadn't been able to reach Keenan, and she assumed that he wasn't overjoyed she was coming. She found it a touch overdone, however, for him to snub her in favor of a walrus stomach.

Stepping backward so he could enter, she looked more closely at the Bailey man. At first glance he'd seemed all parka and beard. She saw now that he must be preternaturally lean under the bearish coat, and that the beard, well-trimmed, was not as intimidating as she'd first thought. But it gave him a slightly demonic look, an air of danger.

Behind the beard, his face was impassive, unreadable, but not particularly friendly. What registered most strongly was the sheer steadiness of his eyes. He had the bluest eyes she'd ever seen, amazing, a true sky blue. He kept them narrowed, and they seemed to stare right through her. It disquieted her.

Hal was disquieted himself. He hadn't expected a woman like this. Tall and shapely, she stood there in gray wool slacks, a heavy rose-colored sweater, and ski boots. The only ornamentation she wore was a small pink ribbon tied at the end of her braid. Her hair was so gold it seemed to shine with a life of its own.

Brubecker had merely told him "a big blonde." He'd said nothing about a woman so stunning she practically glowed. But Hal also remembered that Brubecker said she was really only a kid who'd played through four years of college, whose specialty was being carefree, and who had never had a real responsibility in her life. Still, she was a stunner.

"Come in," she said, not showing any more friendliness than he did. "Sit down. I'll repack."

He stepped inside, automatically stripping off his heavy parka. Underneath he wore a navy-blue sweater with leather patches at the elbows.

He sat in the room's brown and yellow easy chair and looked around so that he wouldn't stare at the blonde. The bed had an orange spread, and the matching drapes framed a frosted window. A picture of a snow goose in flight hung on the wall.

She began packing things back into her suitcase with military precision. "To tell the truth, I'll be glad to get out of here," she said, not looking at him. "This place is weird. It looks like any hotel room in America. It's hard to believe it's practically sitting on the North Pole. It's amazing."

For a moment he was surprised she would notice. Then he shrugged. What had she expected? An igloo? A bedspread of caribou skins?

He watched the golden braid swinging down her back. It could take on a hypnotic motion that he didn't like. "Listen," he said, "I'd have come for you even if Brubecker had been around. He wants me to talk to you."

She stopped repacking. She turned and looked at him. Again she had the uneasy sensation that he could see right through her. Men were usually intimidated by her, by her height or her name or her money. This one wasn't, and it put her off balance. "Talk to me?"

He fixed his eyes on the print of the snow goose and wondered how he had ever gotten into this. It was all emotional stuff, and Hal was a man of logic. That, of course, was why Brubecker had asked him—he'd wanted someone who would stay rational, cool.

"Brubecker knows why you're here." He made his voice as stern as possible. "But you've got to understand that he's not interested in you romantically. He said to tell you he thinks of you as a sister." There. He'd said it. At least part of it. If everybody was lucky, she'd bawl and stamp her foot, then demand to go back to the airport to catch the next plane home.

She straightened up to her full height. It was impressive. She put a hand on her hip. "I don't need you to tell me there's nothing between us. What is this?"

He ignored her accusing stare and stroked his mustache. "He doesn't want you getting your hopes up, that's all. He considers his relationship to you strictly friendly. You're welcome as long as you know that. If you have to write about something, he says to write about the work we're doing here. Arctic research could use some good press."

Stunned, she stared at him. Humiliation surged through her, followed quickly by anger. The man was infuriating, sitting there so coolly, not even bothering to look at her. "Are you out of your mind?" she demanded. "Is he out of his? Who does he think—"

Hal cut her off. He didn't want to hurt the girl, but somebody had to, and the job had fallen to him. "Look. He knows you think you're in love with him. He's sorry. But he's found someone else. He's getting married. He's told his grandfather, but the old man won't listen."

"He *what*?" demanded Jen. Her cheeks turned as pink as her sweater. "Would you please *look* at me when you talk to me? Could you show me that much courtesy?"

He swung his gaze to meet hers, and she wished she hadn't asked for his attention. Looking into those eyes was like walking off the edge of the earth and falling into pure sky. She got a strange, fluttering feeling in the pit of her stomach. *Keenan, what have you done to me?* she thought numbly.

Hal forged on, determined to be done with it. "Keenan's proposed and she's accepted. He figured his grandfather wouldn't believe he was serious, but he is. Her name is Helena Mattak. She's an Inupiat girl. Works at our lab. Very bright girl. Very pretty. Lovely personality. Exceptionally nice woman. Exceptionally."

"Inupiat?" Jen said, not understanding.

Hal held up his hand, as if ordering silence. "She's Eskimo. I know you're hurt, but please don't say anything snobbish that you'll regret. We're all human beings."

He was lecturing her as if she were a child, and Jen hated him for it. She slammed her suitcase shut with a furious motion. "Don't call me a snob," she ordered. "Keenan can marry anybody he wants. And don't you *dare* assume I'm some kind of bigot, you—"

He signaled for her silence with the same curt, maddening gesture. Jen clamped her lips shut in frustration. He was a man like her grandfather, used to being in command, and she'd had her fill of the type.

"She and Brubecker understand each other. You might say he's found himself up here. This is where he intends to stay. So don't even try to think of changing it."

"Men!" Jen pulled the heavy suitcase off the bed and set it on the floor with a resounding thump. "You and Keenan both have a lot of nerve, thinking—"

"I know, I know," he went on, "your pride is hurt. But you're young, you're . . . reasonably attractive, and you'll get over it. In the meantime, we sincerely hope you'll enjoy your stay in Ultima. Welcome to Alaska. I guess I forgot to say that."

"Have you heard anything I've said? One single solitary word?" She put both hands on her hips. She hadn't thought such a thing possible, but this man was more intolerable than Dagobert. She tried to glare him down and failed.

He merely nodded and gave his mustache a restless tug. "Look," he told her, "if you want to go back to the airport—"

"I'm not going back to the airport. I want to talk to Keenan." She would read Keenan the riot act when she saw him. How dare he inflict this condescending man on her? And how dare Ferd and Dagobert send her up here when they knew Keenan loved someone else? Did they really think she would break up someone's romance? Things had to be set straight. "I have to talk to him."

"Like I say, he's gone." Hal sounded infuriatingly calm. "I'll understand if you'd rather stay here than come to the facility. Brubecker just thought you might like to see the research up close and personal. It has the potential for a story—perhaps even for several stories. For instance, right now two whales—"

"Oh, I wouldn't miss it," Jen said between clenched teeth. She took her new powder-blue parka from the closet and shrugged into its depths. "I'm giving Keenan a piece of my mind. I want to see him the minute he gets back. If you'd be good enough to tell me when *that* might be."

She thought that for the first time he looked uncomfortable. "Sooner or later."

She wound a muffler round her neck, pulled on a blue knit cap that matched her parka. "And I'd love to see your precious research—'up close and personal.' After I've come all this way, I might as well see something. What's your particular specialty, Doctor? It's certainly not tact."

He stood, pulling his parka back on. He supposed he should be grateful that she wasn't going to cry. Her anger, however, irritated him. "Whales, Miss Martinson. My specialty is whales."

He picked up her suitcase, then reached for the door at the same moment she did. Their bare hands met. He stepped back from the contact almost as swiftly as she did. Then he reached again and opened the door. He set his jaw, because her hand had felt like silk against his own—far too pleasurable.

Jen was similarly unsettled by the unexpected moment of touching. When her bare fingers brushed against his, the room had seemed to rush in, closing around her. Hal Bailey's shoulders were so bulky in the parka she wasn't sure she could pass through the door without touching him again. Contact with him was as disconcerting as contact with a live wire—it somehow shook the very blood. Her eyes stayed locked with his.

This man was unlike Keenan or the boys in college or the men she worked with on the paper. When he looked at her, it gave her an odd, tingling feeling in the back of her neck. He didn't seem to like her much, and it bothered her more than it should. She didn't want him to know he rattled her, so she set her mouth at an irritated angle. *Don't push me,* her look said. *I can be dangerous if I have to.*

He shrugged, as if her mood was no concern of his. He pulled his fur-trimmed hood up and led her through the lobby, past Sonia's curious black gaze. He had left his truck running, and the cab was warm. The words Arctic Research Facility were stenciled on its battered side.

"You kept this thing running the whole time you were inside?" she asked, settling in beside him.

"That's the way we do things here," he said, switching the headlights on. "Let it run all day sometimes."

"That's wasteful." She found it pleasant to be judgmental.

"It's better than having a frozen engine." He backed the truck up and started east. "Now what's wrong? Why the frown?"

Jen stared at the little graveled main street, as disconcerted by it now as she had been earlier, when she'd arrived. All the buildings looked prefabricated, like boxy toys. They sat on pilings, which made them seem fragile, as if they balanced on thin birdlike legs.

Beyond the buildings, the land threatened to stretch out forever under its thin blanket of snow. Ultima didn't look at all the way she'd imagined a town in the arctic circle would look. They passed a pink building with a large neon sign that said Luigi's Real Italian Pizza. Outside were parked two snow machines and an empty Chevrolet, its motor running full blast. Its exhaust drifted out like a ghost upon the night.

She felt dislocated in space and time, and the lean man next to her had stirred her to anger, as well. She sighed. Anger would do no good. She tried to let it go. "I thought it'd be more—exotic, I guess."

"Yeah," he answered, sounding bored. They left the main street behind and headed down a road that seemed to lead to the snow-covered heart of nowhere. "Most people do."

"I thought I'd see a dog sled, at least," she muttered, unfastening her parka.

"Dog sleds are a thing of the past. A few are around for recreation. It's snow machines now."

Jen stared out at the stark flatness, gnawing her lower lip. "No igloos?"

"Not around here." His tone sounded as if he'd explained the same thing to a hundred people before her. "We don't get that much snow. Houses used to be made of earth. Or skins. Now they're prefab."

Jen shook her head, brooding. "I took a cab from the airport to the hotel. The driver was a native. He was playing Irish rock music on a Japanese tape deck, and the parka he was wearing looked like it came from L.L. Bean."

"The wonders of mail-order shopping." Hal's voice was sardonic.

"No kayaks?"

"Power boats mostly."

"Television even up here?"

"Satellite dishes. Keep a sharp eye out, will you? I saw a polar bear on the way in."

To his surprise, she didn't shudder. She looked out into the vastness with greater scrutiny. "A polar bear would be nice—more what I expected. And penguins, maybe."

A sinister beat of silence told her she'd blundered, but she didn't know how. "Penguins are at the south pole," he said at last. "Antarctica."

"Oh." If he'd wished to make her feel stupid, he'd succeeded. Geography had never been her strength. Neither had biology, for that matter. She realized she knew nothing about this place, didn't want to, and that she and this man had nothing in common. She might as well be stranded in outer space with an unfriendly Martian.

She lapsed into silence. She had been in Alaska less than a day, yet it frightened her. It was too big. It covered too much space, too many time zones, contained too many contradictory things. In a few hours she had been swept from the modern hustle of Anchorage and over the intimidating peaks of the little-explored Brooks Range.

Now here she was on the far side of those mountains. This vast sweep of land was more like a planet unto itself than a mere state in the union. She looked out into the night and could not see one living thing. The land suddenly seemed to overwhelm her. It was not hostile. It was indifferent, which was worse. She felt like a tiny and fragile spark of life, easily extinguishable.

She sank more deeply into her parka. "Why do people come here?" she asked. "Why do they stay?" She remembered the golden sunshine of California, the blue of its warm ocean.

He was quiet a moment. "Trying to run from something. Or to find something."

"Which are you?" She turned and scrutinized his profile. Once again she thought that the beard made him look slightly devilish. "Running or looking?"

He shrugged. He wished she wouldn't ask so many questions. She made him atypically uneasy. He liked to keep to himself. "I came to see what I could see. When I've seen enough, I'll move on."

He was, she thought, a hard man to figure and one determined to be elusive. "Where are you from?"

"I've worked in Seattle, San Diego. Raised in Indiana."

"And where do you go from here?" The truck hit a dip, and her shoulder accidentally met his. They each pulled away quickly from the contact.

"Next? Maybe Boston. Or Greenland. The South Pacific. Who knows?"

A drifter, she thought, oddly impressed. The kind of man calling no place home. He was the sort who'd always be moving on, looking for a new horizon. No wonder he had an aura of not being quite tame.

"What about you?" he asked at length. "You trying to find anything? Besides Keenan?"

She made her tone curt. "All I want is a story. I didn't come here for Keenan. I don't even think I know him that well. Why'd he come here? To lose something. Or find it?"

"Both, I guess. To lose what's false. To find what's real."

"This doesn't seem real." She looked out at the road stretching toward the darkness. Suddenly, on the horizon to the south, the black sky was visited by a phantom glow of wavering green. It was as if someone had fluttered a veil of ghostly light over the edge of the earth.

It disappeared. Jennifer blinked. The sky was black again, and the stars seemed distant. But then the light returned, a hazy, luminous emerald that seemed to waft across the darkness as if dancing. It pulsed, fading and glowing, then fading and glowing again.

Suddenly the greenish radiance rose high into the sky, then shivered into a deep and delicate yellow toward the bottom, becoming the rare color of the buttercup. "Oh, my," she breathed.

The lights grew more powerful, the color ripening from pale gold into ghostly reds. The scant snow reflected it in pale imitation. "Oh, my," she said again.

Hal pulled to the side of the road, stopping the truck but keeping the motor running. The comfortable thing to do would be to put his arm along the back of the seat behind her, but he did not allow himself to be comfortable. The gesture might seem too friendly, too intimate. He watched her silhouetted against the veils of blushing light.

"Aurora borealis," he muttered. "Northern lights."

He'd let her watch a moment before moving on. He always liked to stop and watch a bit himself. The sight was grand and eerie, and it lifted people out of themselves. Tonight, however, it made him feel odd, empty of everything except restlessness. The lights had come up with unusual suddenness, and if he were a fanciful man, he would almost have thought it an omen. It was as if they had been lying in wait for the appearance of this woman.

Jen sat, dazed, staring at the play of splendor across the dark. She was enchanted, intoxicated.

Her wonder was so intense that it somehow embarrassed Hal. He didn't like to see her showing sensitivity. It went counter to his theories about her and the Martinson family in general. He took refuge in what he knew best, facts. "You're watching atmospheric physics at work. Charged particles from the sun bombard the oxygen and nitrogen in the upper atmosphere—"

Shut up, you jerk, he told himself. He sounded pompous and boring, even to himself.

She said the most unscientific thing possible. She turned to him, her face shining like a kid's. "It's magic."

He studied her. Behind her the curtain of delicate light rippled, pale green falling to rose at the bottom. Her long braid hung over her shoulder. It gleamed faintly, reflecting the hovering lights in the sky.

Her observation disturbed him. He didn't believe in sorcery of any kind and didn't like to contemplate it. "Magic," he grumbled in his beard, putting the truck back into gear. "Right."

He headed down the empty road again, toward the safe, sane, scientific world of the research facility.

He slid her another restless glance. Her face, staring out at the lights, had the rapt expression of a woman in love. She looked radiant enough to wrench a man's heart out of his chest. No wonder Helena was scared to death of her and Keenan hadn't dared face her.

I want this woman out of here, he thought darkly. *As soon as possible.*

Neither of them spoke again until they reached the research facility, a collection of Quonset huts huddled beneath the towering curtain of the lights. He showed her to her room, which was small and barren.

He dropped the key into her hand. "They start serving breakfast as seven hundred hours. I'll pick you up at five to. Be ready." He spoke stiffly, as if his teeth were on edge.

His coldness bewildered her. When he'd stopped on the road, he had seemed almost kind. Then the kindness had vanished, and he'd grown increasingly distant. She gave him a long look, steady and searching. "Why do you dislike me so much?" Her voice was quiet, calm enough to unsettle him even further.

He thought of Brubecker, fleeing from this woman's wiles, and of Helena, frightened of her influence. He thought of the Martinson Corporation and its disregard for the environment. He thought of Bristol Bay and the damage old Martinson would do if he decided to move in. He decided to be honest even if it sounded brutal. "You don't belong here. You're not our kind."

He'd hurt her, he could tell. He told himself he had no choice. Nobody'd asked her here. Nobody wanted her, least of all he. He nodded an unfriendly farewell and started to shut the door.

Jen's pain turned quickly to anger. She was, after all, Dagobert's granddaughter, which meant she had a fighter's spirit.

"Dr. Bailey?" She caught the door, keeping it open. The set of her mouth was militant.

"Yes?"

"You're not my kind, either. You're rude, hostile, and no gentleman."

He gave her a long look of appraisal. She had surprised him. He was not used to people talking back.

Slowly he smiled. It was a smile of condescension. She wasn't about to get the upper hand. The trick, he was sure, was to keep her off balance. He felt a primal male urge to put her in her place and keep her there.

He took her hand from the door and turned down the edge of her glove. She was too surprised to object when he raised her hand to his lips. She could only watch as he bent slightly, his eyes still on hers, and kissed the inside of her wrist. His mouth was warm, and his beard tickled. Her veins seemed to leap insanely beneath the heat of his lips.

He turned the edge of her glove back up and smiled again. "Is that gentlemanly enough? Or should I kneel, too?"

The glint in his narrowed eyes told her he'd never kneel to anyone, man or woman. He dropped her hand.

Jen stared at him in disbelieving fury. Although his lips had barely brushed her skin, the spot throbbed hot and crazy. "You devil," she said between her teeth. "You cold-blooded, arrogant devil."

"Have sweet dreams," said the devil. And he shut the door.

CHAPTER THREE

WHEN HAL KNOCKED at Jen's door at precisely 6:55 a.m., she was scrubbed, dressed, ready and waiting. She sat on the edge of her bed, feeling as isolated as a prisoner in solitary confinement.

Snatching up her purse, she sprang to answer his knock, her braid swinging out behind her. She wore a pair of gray tweed slacks and a white cotton sweater. She unbolted the door and threw it open. Awake for two long hours, she would have been glad to see anyone, even the hostile and unsettling Hal Bailey.

She was startled to see instead a good-looking stranger. A rangy man with wide shoulders looked her up and down, his mouth quirked critically. He had a squared jaw and a chin with a slight cleft in it.

Yet those narrowed blue and steady eyes could belong only to Bailey. What, Jen wondered, had he done to himself? If it weren't for the untamed glitter deep within his gaze, he'd almost look civilized.

Then she realized the beard and mustache were gone. His mouth was fuller and more sensitive than she would have thought. It was, in fact, a handsome mouth, and expressive. What it expressed was impatience.

"What did you do to yourself?" she asked suspiciously. "And why?" She had enough changes to adjust to without discovering that Hal Bailey had a face. He smelled faintly of after-shave: the musky scent of De Rothschild. She would not have expected that, either.

"I shaved."

"Why?" Her heart beat fast beneath her demure white sweater. The new Hal Bailey was even more perturbing than the old one.

"I've got a meeting coming up in Anchorage. For grant money." It was as good an answer as any, he supposed irritably. In truth, the meeting wasn't for a month. He'd been shaving, worrying about how he was going to give her the rest of Brubecker's message. Before he'd known it, he'd accidentally shaved off half his mustache. He'd had little choice but to take off everything else. It was aggravating. He should have had his mind on work, not her.

"Well," she murmured, still taken aback, "you look . . . all right, I guess."

"You want breakfast? Or you want to stare at my chin?"

"Breakfast." She gave him a pert look. "I'm just glad you have a chin. A beard can hide a multitude of sins. Like chinlessness."

"Yeah? Well, up here a beard keeps a man warm. And amused. He can let it grow. He can shave it off. Then grow it back again. It passes time. Come on."

With a brusque gesture he ushered her out the door. He wore faded jeans that emphasized his clean muscularity. The sleeves of his blue-and-white striped shirt were rolled back, revealing wrists and forearms of sinewy power.

She glanced away, embarrassed to realize that she'd been staring at him; but he bore himself with an air of coiled power that invited stares. She'd never before met a man even vaguely like him. He seemed as if he might even be a match for Dagobert. The thought intrigued her far more than she liked. She tried to push it away.

"Don't I have to bundle up?" she asked.

"Walkways," he answered. "All these places are connected. Saves time."

She hoisted her shoulder bag more firmly in place and locked the door behind her. Turning, she found herself looking once more into his eyes. A cold jolt vibrated to the center of her bones. He seemed to be standing far too close to her in the narrow hallway. Again she was aware of his tingling musky scent.

"Which way do we go?" Again, staring into his azure eyes, she had the dizzy feeling that she'd fallen off the edge of the earth.

His glance flicked away, took in the empty hall. He nodded his head straight ahead and put his hand on her waist to steer her in the right direction. When he touched her, a spark snapped between them, crackling like a tiny whip. He pulled back swiftly. Jen tensed, startled.

"Static electricity." He moved away, careful to maintain his distance. "These things—build up."

"Of course." She nodded and strode toward the door at the end of the hall, purposeful and businesslike.

He stood for a second, watching how her golden braid swung, its tip brushing the ripe curve of her hips. He rubbed his freshly shaven chin. He reminded himself that he was a reasonable man, who did not allow himself to be battered to and fro by emotion. He set his face stonily and followed her.

The dining room shone with an institutional gleam. Light pulsed down coldly from the fluorescent lamps. Breakfast was being dispensed, cafeteria style, by a stocky man with a drooping black mustache. He stood behind the stainless steel counter, resplendent in his white uniform and apron. Hal called him Arnold.

Arnold had the bronzed skin, pronounced cheekbones and dark eyes of a native. He looked at Jen without a glimmer of curiosity. When she smiled at him, he didn't smile back; he simply filled her plate and handed it to her.

Hal led Jen to a square table with a Formica top. At first they were alone in the room, except for Arnold. They ate in uncomfortable silence.

People began drifting into the dining hall singly and in pairs. All were men. They said hello to Hal and stared with frank curiosity at Jen. Hal nodded back without comment. The men took the hint and sat apart, darting furtive glances toward Jen.

Nobody came near them. It was as if Hal emitted threatening vibrations that warned others away.

"Why don't you introduce me or something?" she whispered across the table. "This is uncomfortable. Am I the only woman here?"

"I'll introduce you later." In fact, he hoped he wouldn't have to introduce her at all, that she would be long gone by noon. "There are two women—they usually eat later. Most of the senior scientists who aren't married live here. Relax."

Jen couldn't relax. Being in this room of staring men made her feel as if she were trapped in a submarine with a cargo of lumberjacks. Most of the men were hefty and bearded. One of them leered openly at her until Hal stared him down. It took, she noted, approximately five seconds for Hal Bailey to stare a man down and keep him that way.

At last a young native man with an irrepressible gleam in his eyes entered the room and flashed Hal a grin. He filled his tray and came to their table.

He slapped Hal on the back and Hal flinched, not at the discomfort, but at the familiarity. He was in no mood to fraternize. He had too many problems, and the blonde was the least of them.

"Hey! Dr. Bailey," the young man said. He had on a red knit shirt with a small green alligator ornamenting the chest. Without invitation, he placed his tray on the table and sat down.

Smiling, he thrust his hand out at Jen. "Hi," he said, his English accented. "I'm Billy Owen. You must be Brubecker's friend. Miss Martinson?"

Hal frowned into his coffee, but Jen took Billy's proffered hand with gratitude. At least he'd had the decency to call her "Brubecker's friend," not "Brubecker's blonde." And he was courageous enough to brave Hal's hostility and attempt friendliness.

"Call me Jen." She decided she could like Billy Owen. He looked as if he came at life from a merry angle. He had a square, clean-shaven face and extremely black eyes, bright behind horn-rimmed glasses.

"So what's with you?" he said, turning to Hal. "Where did your whiskers go? Now you're all smooth in the face, like the pretty boys on TV. Next thing I know, you be selling shaving creams in the ads."

Jen smiled in spite of herself, and Hal frowned harder into his coffee. "Aren't you here early? Don't you eat at home?"

Billy flashed his white grin at Jen. "This morning I come early. To see what I can see. It was worth the trouble, believe me."

"What do you do here?" Jen asked, grateful for someone willing to talk.

"I work. I'm his assistant." He pointed to Hal without the least reverence. "I'm taking a year off before I finish college. I'm going to be a big shot biologist, like him. Only I, of course, will be charming."

Jen laughed.

"Billy," Hal barked, unsmiling, "*quiet*. When you're through here, go check the equipment. We've got to go out on the ice."

The smile died on the young man's face.

Hal stood abruptly. He gave Jen a cold nod. "Come on." He strode off. She tried to give Billy a sympathetic glance, but he was embarrassed and wouldn't meet her eyes.

She threw down her napkin, pushed back her chair and rose. To be civil, she would have to follow Hal. But it rankled her to be polite when he didn't make the slightest effort to do so himself.

Not bothering to speak, he led her through a maze of corridors and walkways. "Why were you so short tempered with that boy?" she asked, trying to keep up. "It was nice of him to be friendly."

"He was too friendly. He was being fresh. He was showing off for you. You were encouraging him. You shouldn't. He's got a lot to learn."

"About what? How to bow down to *you*? Excuse me, your worship, I didn't realize I was in the presence of one so mighty."

He stopped at a door much like all the other doors in the corridor. A rectangular brass plate announced his name and title: Dr. Harold K. Bailey, Director.

He tossed her an unfriendly glance. He was tired of her complicating his already complicated life. She not only threatened his peace, but Keenan and Helena's. "Your grandfather sent you to fancy schools. Didn't they teach manners? Wait—I remember. You were too busy—what was it—surfing? Skiing?"

He unlocked his door. She felt her cheeks burn. She would have gleefully consigned him to blazes. So he thought she was some prep school prig or beach bunny, did he?

She followed him into his cluttered office, her heart thudding in rebellion. Charts covered his walls, and a computer sat on a desk littered with papers, printouts, folders and maps.

"I wouldn't talk about manners, if I were you," she said.

He stood before his desk, ignoring her. He opened a folder, staring down at it. He was going to have to tell her the rest of the truth, and he dreaded the task. She was a maddening woman, and had thrown even a man as reasonable as himself temporarily off track. He needed a moment to tune her out of his consciousness.

She refused to be tuned out. She stepped to the edge of his desk, turning so that she looked into his face. "And the schools I went to weren't particularly fancy. I may not have been the world's best student, but my grandfather taught me one important thing—not to be easily impressed."

He flicked her a brief glance that told her he was not impressed, either. It only made her angrier.

"You may be the lord-high muckey-muck of this godforsaken place—" she threw her arm out to indicate the facility "—but that doesn't—excuse the expression—cut any ice with me."

His blue eyes went as cold as human eyes can go. "You're like him, you know that?"

"Like who?" she demanded. He had edged dangerously close to her, but she refused to retreat.

"Like that kid," he answered with contempt. "Billy. Neither one of you knows how the word really works. But he's got an excuse. You don't. Now you're blocking my desk drawer. Will you move? Or do I move you?"

Jen, her blood running high, stood her ground. "What do you mean 'how the world really works?' What kind of condescending crack is that?"

"I asked you to move." His jaw muscles were tight.

"I asked for an answer."

He slapped the folder shut, leaned an inch nearer to her. "Billy's a good kid. But he's caught between two cultures, two ways of life. The Eskimos are traditionally a polite people, reticent. Sometimes, like today, Billy bends too far the other way. He goes too far. He's got to learn the rules—when they can be broken and when they can't. Or he'll never get what he wants."

Jen stared at him with disdain. "I see. He didn't treat the great white chief with proper deference. And you called *me* a snob."

"Listen. It doesn't matter if I'm white or green. I'm in charge. That's how it is. In ten years he may be in charge...but only if he knows the rules. Nobody with any sense smarts off to the boss. Especially in front of a visitor."

"You're arrogant."

"You're naive," he answered. "You can afford to be spoiled and mouthy. Billy can't. He's got to make it on his own."

She drew herself up to her full height. That intimidated most men. Hal Bailey wasn't fazed. "I'm not spoiled," she said. "You don't know anything about me."

He sucked in a deep breath between his teeth. "I know enough. You come from a world as remote as Billy's. Just as isolated. And just as divorced from the mainstream. You don't know anything about reality. And, unlike Billy, you don't have to learn. Now, move, will you?"

Firmly he took her by the upper arms and moved her from his desk. He exerted a surprising amount of force and did it so expertly that she felt no pain, only amazement at finding herself shunted aside so easily. Her back was pressed against his overloaded bookcase, and his hands seemed to flame through the sleeves of her sweater, scalding her flesh.

He didn't release her. He seemed determined to make sure she stayed exactly where he intended. He suddenly seemed taller than before. A muscle jerked in his cheek.

"How dare you say..." she began to demand.

His fingers tightened. The blue eyes looked straight through her and seemed to find nothing worthy of regard. "You haven't lived. You've only played. And your grandfather's money makes it possible for you to keep right on playing. It's oil money, Miss Martinson. I don't much like what the oilmen have done to Alaska. Now word is out that your family wants to grab still more of it—Bristol Bay. I don't like that, either."

Her heart seemed lodged in her throat, almost choking her. "I'm not responsible for my grandfather. And he's improved his environmental policies—he's had to."

"He hasn't improved them enough. Everybody who loves Alaska wants to keep Dagobert Martinson out of Bristol Bay. You and your grandfather need to learn that you can't have everything you want. That includes Keenan. Leave him and Helena alone. Let them get on with their life."

Her breath had become so shallow it hurt to breathe. "I see," she managed to say.

"Miss Martinson," he said with elaborate formality, "I seriously doubt that you do. Go back to San Francisco. Tell both your families that Keenan's not for sale."

The muscle in his jaw twitched again. He glanced at his watch. He turned from her and opened the desk drawer she had blocked. He took out a large yellow envelope.

"Here," he said, thrusting it at her and nodding toward an empty chair. "Reporters deal with facts. The facts are here. Keenan's married. He got married last night."

She looked at him, her mouth dropping open. She couldn't breathe at all now. She felt dazed, almost stupified. When she took the envelope, only enormous willpower kept her hands from shaking.

"Keenan's . . . married?" She sat down weakly.

He leaned against his desk, crossing his arms. He kept his face stern. In truth, he was angrier at himself than at her. Brubecker had asked him to break the news gently to the girl, and he'd done a lousy job of it, just a stinking job.

Now, he thought grimly, *now she's going to cry. Nice job, Bailey. And you, Brubecker, do your own dirty work next time, dammit. I don't like hurting women. Even rich, spoiled ones.*

In some crazy way, he thought in frustration, she did remind him of Billy Owen. She'd be a good kid if she could just understand that she wasn't the one making the rules.

Jennifer searched his face for the smallest trace of sympathy and found none. He was enjoying this, she thought with sinking heart. She felt his unwavering gaze as she opened the yellow envelope. She drew out a sheet of paper covered with Keenan's distinctive spidery scribble.

Dear Jen,
I'm sorry to do this by letter, but thought it would be easiest. I'll be married by the time you read this. I'd hoped to make a clean break with you when I left California. This time it must be final. Please believe that what you feel for me isn't love, but only admiration and infatuation.

Admiration? Infatuation? For Keenan? Jen thought in dismay. *Keenan of all people?*

In the meantime, I hope you'll use the wonderful opportunity that's fallen into your hands. There are many fascinating subjects for news stories in the arctic, and I hope you'll take full advantage. (Our recent discoveries about the digestive enzymes of the walrus would make a most interesting feature! There is also an unusual situation concerning two whales that you should ask Dr. Bailey about.)

I will always think of you as a friend.

Regards
Keenan

PS—I'm releasing the story of our elopement to the press. I thought it would be too painful for you or my family to have to do so. Again, best wishes.

Stunned, Jen reread the letter, her disbelief mounting. She could no longer stop her hands from shaking. They trembled with the ardent desire to wrap around Keenan's conceited neck and throttle him.

Slowly she raised her eyes to lock with Hal Bailey's. "Do you know what this says?" She was so humiliated that her voice quavered.

He nodded. Keenan had sweated over the letter for hours. That man was the sort who could face a polar bear with equanimity, but a difficult social situation made him fidget like a cornered mouse.

Jen took a deep breath, trying to calm herself. She stared down at the letter in wonderment. Then she looked up at Hal again, blinking hard.

This is it, he thought grimly. *She's going to cry.* He reached for the tissue box and handed it to her.

"Go ahead. Cry." His voice was gruff. "I'll understand. We thought it best if you learned things a little at a time. I'm sorry I was blunt. I didn't mean to be rude. I—this hasn't been a job I relished. I could have done better."

Jen looked at him without comprehending. She wondered why he was offering her the tissues. Did he really think she was going to *cry*?

She smiled crookedly. "He got married. And he really thinks I want him—that—that fussbudget—"

"What?" Hal looked dubious. He offered her the tissues again.

She waved them away. "He really thinks I want to marry him." She laughed a short, mirthless sound. "And he convinced you, too. Everybody around here probably thinks so—even poor Helena. Now they'll think he's jilted me or something—*Keenan*?"

Hal winced. The way the girl acted, she must be in some kind of shock.

The slightly crooked smile stayed pasted on Jen's lips. "How could I love *Keenan*?"

"It's perfectly reasonable," Hal said. "He's an excellent biologist. A fine man. Serious. Earnest. You've known him all your life. He's got money. And both your families want it."

"He's *boring*," Jen said in anger and dismay. "When we'd go to the beach, he'd spend the whole time with his nose in a tide pool, watching sea urchins."

Hal eyed her doubtfully. Was she trying to console herself with the old sour-grape psychology? Since she couldn't have Keenan, she'd enumerate his faults?

Jen kept shaking her head in wonder. "He's shorter than I am. He hates the sun—it gives him prickly heat. I mean, he's a nice man. He's been very kind to me, and I told him I was fonder of him than anybody I knew. He's a nice, shy, fussy old teddy bear, but I never said I *loved* him. I said I hoped we'd always be close, but I never said I wanted to *marry* him."

She looked at Hal as if expecting him to clear her of the senseless accusation that she could love Keenan. "And now he's run off and gotten married," she said. "I wish him every happiness, but I hope—" She shook her head in concern. "He really does love Helena, doesn't he? And she loves him?"

Hal nodded. "He loves her. He'd told his grandfather he was going to marry her, but the old man wouldn't accept it. He sent you. So they upped the date."

She gave another humorless laugh. "I'm practically Cupid. And I bet he's not coming back here until I'm gone, is he?"

Hal didn't like the gleam of laughter in her eyes. "No. I gave them honeymoon leave. They won't be back for three weeks. Look, I'll be blunt. He doesn't want to see you. He wants to get on with his marriage and his life."

"And in the meantime, you're stuck with me. And you hope I'll leave, too. You hate every minute of this. And you don't like me."

His expression darkened. Things shouldn't have gotten personal with the girl, but somehow they had, deeply personal, right from the start. "It's best if you go. Frankly, the arctic isn't the best place for somebody named Martinson to make friends. Your grandfather's not popular here. Am I clear enough for you?"

She laughed again. "Clear as crystal. Gee—last week I was just a harmless drudge for the society page of the paper. Now Keenan thinks I'm stalking him, and you think I'm a barbarian princess, living off Dagobert's spoils. I didn't realize I had this dark, sinister side."

Her face went pensive once more. "What I can't forgive is that he didn't let me break the story. The first time in my life I've found a decent story—and he doesn't even let me have it. He's announced it already, hasn't he?" She looked at her watch. "You timed it, didn't you, to make sure he'd have announced it before I knew."

Hal nodded.

She shook her head. "So I—the fearless reporter—am the last to know. Oh, this is one for the books. Is this why there was no phone in my room?" she asked. "There's a jack, but no phone. I wasn't supposed to communicate with the outside world till Keenan was married—and safe from me."

She rose, trying to keep from laughing again. The joke wasn't just on her. It was on her grandfather, as well. And old Ferd Brubecker. Even on Keenan, who had sadly misread her intentions. Even on Hal Bailey, who stood by his desk, his face impassive.

Her knees felt unsteady, her brain a bit giddy, but she had a dazzling sense of freedom, far stronger and more intoxicating than she'd felt back in San Francisco. Nobody could ever again insist that she marry Keenan. Keenan had set them both free.

The universe was absurd, it was an immensely funny joke, and Jen felt almost faint with the hilarity of it.

Hal stepped in front of her, looking more forbidding than ever. "Where do you think you're going?"

"Anchorage." She gave him the smile she couldn't quite make steady. "I'm going to look for a job. I told my grandfather I wasn't coming home, and I meant it. I won't wait here for Keenan. I'm obviously an embarrassment to him. It's time we got on with our separate lives."

"Are you all right?" he demanded. "You're not going to faint are you?"

She gave another of those small breathless laughs he found so ominous. She shook her head. She tapped him on one shoulder with Keenan's letter, as if she were knighting him for some splendid deed. "Thanks for the hospitality. You're going to make it a real pleasure to be alone."

He gave her such a scathing look that she couldn't stop herself. She raised herself on tiptoe slightly and let her lips graze his. "Thanks a million." She started to laugh again.

She was startled when his arms shot around her so swiftly that she found herself imprisoned in them. His hard chest pressed against her breasts, and his lips stayed closed to hers, so close that they nearly touched. She blinked in alarm. Although she was young and strong, he was infinitely stronger, an extraordinarily powerful man.

"You're not alone," he said roughly. "You're all right."

His arms held her so inescapably she could hardly breathe. His warmth and the scent of his cologne made her feel slightly drunk. "I'm alone and I like it," she objected. "Stop looking so serious. This is funny, really—I could laugh and laugh—"

"I said you're not alone. Don't get hysterical. Get control of yourself."

She felt even giddier than before, crushed as close to him as she was. Her lips tingled from the brief touch against his. She was filled with strange emotions, all soaring and sailing. She could not help smiling, even though he held her captive. She *liked* being in his arms. How odd, she thought. Another joke the universe was playing.

He stared down at her, his face severe. It was worse than he feared—she was going to fly apart before his eyes. "Take a deep breath. Things will be fine. You can go home to your job and your grandfather."

"No. I've as good as quit the job. My grandfather has to learn he can't run my life. I'm going to Anchorage. Or maybe Fairbanks. Which is nicer?"

"Face reality," he ordered.

"I can't find it," she said and laughed. "None of this can actually be happening." She fought the irrational desire to put her arms around his neck.

"Don't laugh. Doesn't anything ever seem real to you?" he asked, almost angry.

She nodded. She felt she was drifting away. Everything in the world did seem unreal, except for the man who held her so tightly in his arms. "You," she said. "You're real, I think."

The look in his eyes changed. Something in the way he held her altered subtly. He lowered his head. She thought he was going to kiss her. She was amazed to find she wanted him to. She closed her eyes.

"No," he said. "That's a game I won't play."

Her eyes snapped open. His mouth was only an inch from hers, but its set was fierce. "What?" she asked.

"You feel rejected. But don't try to use me to prove you don't care about him. I'll help you if I can. But I don't play games."

Her giddiness evaporated. Her smile died. "No wonder you and Keenan both came here. You have such colossal egos, Alaska's the only place they'd fit."

A knock at his door jarred them both. She sprang backward, and he let his arms fall away from her. "Sit down," he muttered. "You're not going anywhere. You're not acting rationally. First you're hysterical, then you're seductive . . ." He shook his head in exasperation.

She sat down again, no longer trusting her legs. Maybe the universe had become a bit too absurd. She knew she wasn't trying to be seductive, but she couldn't think quite straight, either. Her thoughts and emotions were all tumbled together.

Again the knock rattled the door. Hal pushed his hand through his hair and flung the door open. He looked down into Billy Owen's once-more amiable face. "What? Are you ready? I'll be there in a minute."

As if through a haze, Jen heard Billy saying something about whales. Whales trapped in the ice.

Billy shook his head. "The Federal guy finally called. He left word at the central office. He'll be here in three days, if things aren't any better."

Jen stared at the boy numbly. She had no idea what he was talking about.

Billy looked suddenly worried. "Me, I don't think they should be destroyed. I've got a funny feeling about this whole thing. I'm not superstitious. But did you see how weird the lights were last night? It was spooky, man. My grandmother says strange things are coming on, some very strange forces are being set loose. I kind of believe it."

Hal started to rebuke Billy for being unscientific, but stopped himself. He'd been too hard with the kid earlier this morning, and he regretted it. Besides, he'd learned long ago that the Inupiat knew things about the North that science had yet to learn.

"We'll check the situation. Bring the truck to the east entrance in five minutes."

Billy threw a curious look at Jen, then nodded and closed the door.

Hal turned wordlessly and looked at her. She was still pale, still shaky.

"What's happening?" she asked.

There was a beat of silence between them. They looked into each other's eyes warily. "We've got two young gray whales trapped in the ice. Something's going to have to be done."

She frowned. She'd heard of whales being stranded, but never in the ice. "What will you do?"

He'd been so swept up in Keenan's fool problems, he'd almost been able to forget about the whales. Now the real world closed around him again, hard as iron.

"I don't know." He turned from her again and studied the meteorological forecasts on his desk. They weren't promising, but neither were they hopeless. He would have to act according to the way the weather acted, take his cues from the ice.

Once more he wished the woman were gone. She was too damned distracting, but he supposed he'd have to keep her with him awhile, at least until she got her bearings back. "I'll take you to see them," he said, his voice almost kind. "Maybe you can write about them. Maybe somebody somewhere will be interested."

His expression had gone worried, almost haggard. She knew the situation must be serious indeed.

The poor whales, she thought; their plight sounded terrible. What an unbearable fate, to be caught in the ice, unable to go home again.

"Do you really think anybody will care?" she asked. "About the whales, I mean?"

He shook his head. He supposed he had no business letting her get her hopes up again. He'd told her to face reality. She could start now. "No. Nobody'll care. Not really."

She looked at the stony set of his expression. It was so serious it made her heart constrict. "Do you care? About what happens to them?"

He gave her a measuring glance. "They're a problem to solve. That's what I'm paid to do." He shrugged one shoulder and turned his attention back to his reports.

Jen, still shaken, regarded him uneasily. She was not sure what emotions, if any, lay behind those unwavering eyes. Perhaps he truly was a man so cold and clinical that he didn't care about the suffering of a pair of trapped whales.

Or perhaps, she thought, just perhaps, he was one who cared so deeply he could not speak of it, one whose feeling ran so passionately that he kept it locked safely away from public view. For an instant she had an intuition that he was a far more volatile man than he seemed, one whose commitment, once pledged, could be almost fierce.

No, she told herself, that couldn't be. She should not even imagine that there were things Hal Bailey could care about.

CHAPTER FOUR

SHE SAT, miserable, swathed in her winter gear, squeezed in the truck between Hal and Billy Owen. Hal had said, "I want to keep an eye on you. I'm not leaving you alone in the shape you're in."

She almost cringed at the memory. *He not only thinks I'm a spoiled brat in love with Keenan, he also thinks my heart is broken, and I'm on the verge of being hysterical or crazy with despair.*

The Arctic stretched around them, flat as the plains of Nebraska, its sky the streaked and eerie blue of early dawn.

"What did you mean, the whales are probably doomed?" she asked, glancing at Hal's angular profile. He wore a parka of brownish gold.

He shrugged and didn't answer, lost in his own unpleasant mood. He wanted the girl to leave, yet until he was sure of her emotional state, he didn't dare to let her go, nor did he think he should leave her alone. Now that he had her, however, he wished he didn't. He had expected a very she-devil of an heiress. He had something else instead, but he wasn't sure what. It made him edgy.

When Hal said nothing, Billy spoke. He looked at Jen over the rims of his horn-rimmed glasses. For a moment he resembled the serious scientist he hoped to become.

"These are California gray whales. They summer here. They should have migrated back south already."

She nodded. She understood that.

Billy went on. "These two didn't go soon enough. A hunter found them. They're frozen in. All they got left's a breathing hole. And it's getting smaller."

"You mean they'll die there?" Jen was horrified.

Billy nodded. "Could be. They can't survive in the ice. The bowhead whales could. They're built for the Arctic. They could punch right up through the ice, make new breathing holes. Get back to the open sea. These can't."

"That's terrible," she said.

"That's the Arctic. Only the strong survive."

Although she was warm in her blue parka, Billy's words made her shiver. She looked out at the alien landscape. It was nearly ten o'clock in the morning, and the sun was just rising. To Jen's astonishment, it was rising in the south.

The road from the facility had quickly given way to nothingness, and she found herself being jolted first over the frozen earth, then over a white sea as solid as stone.

Billy, who obviously enjoyed being the source of information, filled Jen in on the details. The whales had been found by a hunter scouting for sign of seal. The hunter, a middle-aged man named Warren Tipana, was an Eskimo from Ultima and Billy's uncle.

The whales were young, they were not very big—one was only thirty feet long, the other even less. An adult gray could reach forty or even fifty feet.

Billy shook his head at the misfortune of it all. These were foolish young whales who had stayed too long, playing and feeding. Now, unless the ice broke up or shifted, they would pay the ultimate price for their folly. They were trapped miles from any path to the open sea.

Their breathing hole was still clear, but they had battered their noses, cutting them on the ice looking for a way to escape.

As soon as the whales had been reported to Hal, he had gone with Billy, Keenan and Warren Tipana to see what could be done. The men had used chain saws to cut two new breathing holes leading toward the sea, but the whales, apprehensive, refused to move to them.

The animals were obviously stressed, Billy said, they seemed to know they were caught with no way out. Their breathing hole was small, perhaps thirty-five feet by twenty. They had to gulp air with their snouts poking almost straight up. Their meat would be no good to eat, he said, even if gray whales were worth eating in the first place.

"Eat?" Jen cried, appalled. Her response was so abrupt she made the boy jump. She felt Hal tense beside her. "You can't eat a gray whale—it's illegal—they're an endangered species."

"So is Warren Tipana," Hal answered, breaking his silence. "And ninety percent of the people of Ultima."

"A good point," muttered Billy, looking suddenly moody.

Jen glanced suspiciously at the boy, then at Hal. "What do you mean?"

"I mean," Hal said, staring out at the flatness stretching around them, "that the Eskimos lived here for five thousand years. By hunting. They created one of the most unique cultures in the world. Now, after all those centuries, it's dying. A way of life is disappearing."

Jen squirmed a bit. "Well, still, nobody can kill a gray whale and eat it. They're protected."

Hal gave her a cool sidelong glance. "The people in Ultima have always been hunters. The village grew where it did because of the whales. For people to survive here, they had to hunt. They still do. The International Whaling Commission allows them so many whales a year. This year they were allotted a certain number of bowheads. And a quota of grays, as well."

"Wait a minute," Jen objected. "You mean it's actually legal to hunt those poor whales?"

"It's legal to harvest them." Billy's dark eyes met hers. "People have to live. They have to eat. We take no more than law allows."

Jen started to object again, but something in Billy's face stopped her. He was proud of his heritage, proud of the five thousand years his people had endured in this harsh land. She had no right to criticize a culture simply because it was different from hers. Of course the Inupiat had always hunted. No crops could grow here, it was not possible.

She saw Hal eyeing her with that sidelong glance again. *Don't be judgmental,* his gaze said. *You don't begin to understand this place or these people.*

Don't be judgmental yourself, her own eyes replied. *You don't begin to understand me, either.*

But the Arctic suddenly seemed more complex than she had imagined. She thought of the endangered whales, struggling to endure. She thought of the Eskimos, their culture wrenched by outside forces, struggling to adjust and carry on. She thought of oil companies like Dagobert's, battling to dominate nature and changing everything that they touched, even in this far-flung place.

Only the strong survive, she thought, remembering Billy's words. Once more she was aware of Hal Bailey beside her, silent and full of intensity. He was designed for survival here, strong and cold as the land itself.

They parked and started unloading the truck. Carrying equipment, they walked out farther on the frozen sea. They had traveled, Billy said, nine and a half miles from the research facility.

Now they crossed the ice toward a barely perceptible dark spot, a mile distant. If it was the breathing hole, Jen could glimpse it only now and then, for a ridge in the ice hid it from sight for most of their journey.

A slight wind stirred the air, the sky was an achingly beautiful blue, and the temperature, although it nipped at Jen's cheeks, was not nearly as cold as she'd have thought.

A powder of snow covered the blue-white ice, and in the distance the sea gleamed, dark blue and jeweled with great chunks of floating ice. They scrambled over the ridge, and she walked fast to keep stride with the two men as they covered the last twenty feet separating them from the ice hole.

Her resentment vanished when the dark water gave a mighty surge. Suddenly a shape rose into the air. It was huge, as tall as a man and as broad as three men. A triangle of spray rainbowed above it, as a great gasping noise rasped and sighed.

Jen stopped short. Automatically she reached for Hal and squeezed his arm tightly. Her heart shook with a combination of fear and awe.

What she saw was the head of a gray whale, its snout scarred with cuts from the ice. Its eye was small compared to its bulk, but incredibly sad, wise, and human. The gasping was the creature's breathing.

"Good heaven," she heard herself say. She clutched Hal's arm more tightly still. He put his gloved hand over hers. She stood transfixed, watching the trapped giant rear its head above the water, listening to the labor of its breath.

Before she had time to recover from the shock, there was another surge, and a smaller head appeared behind the first. Its dark snout was speckled with barnacles and scratched by ice, its great mouth was set in the sad smile she knew was peculiar to the gray whale. Its eye seemed to take in Jen, to observe her with wariness.

It breathed with a huge, slow panting that tore at her emotions. The animals were huge, but their toiling respiration made them seem fragile. Only air could keep them alive, and they had only this tiny patch of open water in which to find air.

She looked beyond the trapped whales. The closest opening into the sea gleamed miles away. The animals could never find their way to it in the airless dark under the ice. Even if they used the new breathing holes, they could not make it. It was too far for them to swim without coming up for air.

Hal shook his head as he watched the two creatures raising their snouts in the cold air. Although his hand still covered Jen's, he seemed to have forgotten her. He spoke softly to the whales. "You guys are in trouble. Big trouble. And the worse part is that you know."

He swore softly. He brushed Jen's hand away from his arm absently, as if he had hardly noticed it. He knelt by the ragged edge of the hole in the ice. The larger of the whales regarded him, then with a heave it moved toward him.

It's panicking, Jen thought in fright, and it's going to try to kill him. She flinched back from the animal, but Hal did not. To her amazement, the whale simply swam to the edge of the ice and seemed to look at the man.

She did not quite believe it when Hal reached out and touched the creature, stroking it. It bobbed, seeming to evaluate the man's touch. "Buddy," Hal said, petting it with long gentle strokes, "you should have gone south. You're polar bear bait here, unless this ice shifts."

Jen's heart beat hard. She found it difficult to believe that the whale was letting Hal touch it, that it actually seemed to want his touch. It was as if the man and creature had spoken in some mystical way she couldn't hear.

Then the whale drew a last ragged intake of air and disappeared below the surface of the water. A few seconds later the smaller whale followed. The water quieted in a moment. It was as if the whales had never been there.

Hal rose and turned, his face solemn. "Get the camera ready," he said to Billy. "And the hydrophone."

He glanced briefly at Jen, then looked away out toward the horizon. "Well, reporter. What do you think?" He sounded ironical, as though nature had played a trick that both angered and saddened him.

Jen, confounded, tried to regain control of her emotions. She hadn't acted like a reporter when the whales appeared. She'd forgotten about her camera, even her notebook. Of all the sights she'd ever seen, the trapped animals were the most amazing and the most disturbing.

Billy scrambled to prepare the equipment. Jen simply stood, staring into the empty water. It seemed impossible that the great creatures were hidden under its surface.

"Can they find their way back? We haven't frightened them away?"

"They've got no place else to go." Hal nodded at the far-away crack in the ice. "You can see how far it is to a lead to the open sea."

"It let you touch it," she murmured.

"Some of them will."

She nodded numbly. Hal watched the bewildered play of emotions race across her face and seemed to relent a bit. "They're curious, they're intelligent, and they've got a highly developed sense of touch. If they let you touch them once, they usually come back for more."

"That big crack in the ice out there," she said, looking at the distant break that opened toward the sea. "There's not a chance they can make it that far, is there?"

He took the minicam from Billy. "That's called a lead. This ice shifts all the time. A new lead might open for them. You can't predict what happens."

"They might have a chance if it doesn't get colder," Billy added, checking the 35 millimeter camera.

Jen looked at the boy, her face clouding with concern. "What do you mean. This is the Arctic. Of course it'll get colder."

Hal gave Billy a warning look. This was a taste of the real life he had told Jen about, but he didn't want her to get emotional over the situation. It would do no good. Yet it perplexed him that she seemed more disturbed over the whales than she had by the news Keenan was married.

He answered for the boy. "It's been unusually cold all summer, all fall. That's probably how these guys got trapped. If the cold breaks, then they've got a chance."

She turned away, looking back toward the frozen land. "A chance? That's all?"

"It's possible. Just barely."

She stared into the dark water. It sparkled in the thin sunlight. "And if it doesn't get warmer? What then?"

Hal felt sorry for her, but he wasn't going to lie. "If things get worse, we should put them down. That's why the Federal man is coming. To help us estimate the situation. See if we should put them out of their misery."

"No!" Jen cried. "You can't do that—"

Hal frowned. "We may have to. It may be the kindest thing."

"No!" She realized her denial sounded like that of an upset child, one who cannot accept a cruel reality.

"We have to wait and see." Hal's answer was clipped. She'd never cried over Brubecker, and now he was appalled that she seemed about to cry over the whales.

He stared at the glinting water. He had done all he knew to get the whales to new breathing holes, to lead them closer to freedom. Nothing worked. Nobody in recorded history had ever faced such a problem—there were no precedents, no rules, no hints, no clues on how to solve it. As much as he wanted to save the whales, he did not know if it could be done. It was as simple as that.

"Well, what do you plan to do?" she demanded. "Just stand around and watch?"

He made a sound of impatience. "What do you want me to do? Pick them up and carry them out to sea? This is too bad. I'm sorry it's happened, I hope the weather saves them, but in the meantime, we'll use the situation as best we can."

"Use it how?" she asked, almost belligerently.

Oh, Lord, Hal thought. He never should have brought her out here. She was going to go all emotional on him. He would have to make her understand that even if this wasn't fair, it was the way that life worked.

"Research," he said. "These whales offer a unique opportunity for observation."

"Research." She tossed the word back contemptuously. She dug into her camera bag, but she didn't come out with her camera or her tape recorder or even her notebook. She pulled out a small red Swiss army knife, the sort that contains a dozen different kinds of blades.

She stalked away from the men with their cameras. She made her way down to the far end of the ice hole.

"Stay here," Hal ordered. "You don't know your way around on this ice. It isn't a skating rink. What do you think you're doing?"

She kept walking until she was at the farthest end of the breathing hole. She knelt down and began hacking ineffectually at the edge of the ice with the blade of the jackknife. "While you do your *research*," she called righteously, "I'm going to try to make this hole bigger."

He stared at her in disbelief. There she was, in her sky-blue parka, kneeling on the ice, stabbing away at it for all she was worth. He shook his head. Brubecker was right, she was still just a kid.

Brubecker was right about another thing, too. She didn't have the instincts of a reporter. She wasn't even trying to take intelligent notes on what was a unique scientific phenomenon. Instead she was trying, single-handedly, to free two whales with a jackknife. He fought back the impulse to stalk to her and haul her to her feet, make her face facts. But he didn't trust himself. He just watched. She was a naive, idealistic, softhearted young woman, hacking at the ice, trying to help two creatures as out of their element as she was.

Billy laughed.

"It's not funny," Hal practically snarled. The woman would drive him mad before it was over.

CHAPTER FIVE

SUDDENLY THE LARGER of the two whales appeared again. Its mottled snout parted the water, and it released a plume of spray. It took a long, sad, sighing breath.

It seemed to look Hal directly in the eye.

Hal looked back. He started videotaping for the annals of science. He could not afford to be sentimental. He, Billy, Keenan and Warren had nearly frozen their pants off out here, cutting new breathing holes that the whales wouldn't go near. He'd talked himself hoarse on the phone trying to get the coast guard to send him an ice cutter. He'd called every Federal agency with an interest in whales. No real help was coming. None was likely to come.

There was nothing he could do now except observe and hope for weather warm enough to shift the ice. Nothing, he told himself, despite what any golden girl from California wanted.

Down the ice, her long braid hanging over her shoulder, Jen hammered at the edge of the hole, not caring a fig for science. She worked until almost noon, until her knees and fingers were numb. At last Billy Owen made her get up. She agreed, frustrated and exhausted. She'd broken, bent, or blunted everything on the knife, and cracked the handle as well.

They walked back to the truck, which was still running, and got inside to warm up. Jen's gait was more hobble than walk, and Hal eyed her as if she deserved her limping fate.

They ate a lunch of cheese and crackers, washed down with coffee heavy with sugar and thick with cream. Hal wanted Jen to stay in the warmth of the running truck for the rest of the working day. She refused.

She was too tired to hack at the ice any longer, and she had no weapon left with which to chop. She stood in the cold, watching the whales surface, then dive again. Seeing Hal videotape them and Billy run the hydrophone, she finally remembered she was supposed to be reporting.

Hal shook his head at her idea that the general public would be interested in the plight of the whales. If the story appeared in the newspapers at all, it would be a mere mention.

She should remember gray whales were trapped and died every year in these waters, he told her. This was simply the first time in memory that anyone had seen them caught so. Last spring they'd found the carcasses of three grays that must have been trapped in just this way. Only last week they'd found an old bowhead dead. It was nature's way.

"Don't you *care*?" Jen asked.

He was sitting in the driver's seat, holding a cup of coffee. He stared straight ahead, out toward the breathing holes. "Of course I care." He put sarcastic emphasis on the word *care*. "I wouldn't take this job if I didn't care. But this is a tough environment. Not everything and everybody survives. That's reality. Nobody can change it—not you, me, or anybody."

"Don't you have any feelings? Don't you really think anybody's going to care about these whales?" She knew his attitude was correct for a scientist, but science was for someone without a heart.

"No. Short of biologists or ecologists or the fisheries department." He kept staring out at the ice as if it were a puzzle that defied him all his solutions.

Somebody might care, Jen thought stubbornly. She pulled on her cap and gloves and got out of the truck. She spent the afternoon snapping pictures and using her tape recorder to catch the haunting sounds of the whales' breathing.

She tried to write down information, take accurate and reporterlike notes, but the ink in her pen was frozen. Billy laughed and said that always happened. He lent her a pencil.

She was cold, tired, frustrated, and haunted by the steady reappearance of the whales, who, she imagined, seemed to be asking for help. When she finally got up nerve to try to pet the larger of the two, she was moved when it permitted her caress and returned for another. "Hello, you big goofus." Her voice choked with emotion. "You need to get out of here. You and your doofus buddy."

Billy laughed again and officially christened the whales Goofus and Doofus. Hal, not amused, only shook his head.

Far too early in the afternoon, the sun started to descend. It sank in the same direction from which it arose, the south. Jen, shuddering from the increased chill, realized that the long Arctic night was starting to fall. One day the sun would no longer rise. The breathing holes, the leads to the sea, even the smallest cracks in the ice would freeze over, sealing the whales as if in a tomb.

"Will the hole freeze over tonight?" she asked, as Hal practically forced her into the truck.

"No. They have a while left—probably. Get in."

Reluctantly, clinging to the hope that the weather might open a path to freedom, Jen climbed into the truck's cab.

"You drive," Hal ordered Billy, tossing him the keys. "I want to make sure she's all right. I don't want Brubecker to hear I let his blonde get frostbitten."

"I told you," Jen snapped, her patience exhausted, "I'm not Brubecker's blonde, I'm not anybody's blonde. And I'm fine. Worry about your whales, not me."

He climbed in beside her and picked up the thermos. He made her drink the last of the coffee. In spite of herself, she was grateful for the heat of the cup against her cold fingers, the warm glow that each sip created within her.

Hal took one of her hands and examined it, frowning. "You're flirting with frostbite. How do your feet feel?"

She pulled her hand away and put it back against the warmth of her cup. He ignored the abruptness of the gesture and took her other hand. "Dammit." He rubbed a grayish spot on her wrist, "you really are flirting with it. I said what do your feet feel like?" He kept her wrist, his hand clamped around it so the warmth from his fingers poured into her.

"They don't feel," she muttered. She finished the last of her coffee and suppressed a shudder. Whether it was a delayed shiver from the cold or one triggered by his nearness, she couldn't tell.

"You can't feel them?" He took the cup from her and set it down. "Why didn't you say so?"

"I can feel them *some*," she objected. "They don't hurt, they're just tingly. I'm not stupid. I'd know if I'd needed to get off that ice. I've skied every winter since I could stand up. It's not like I've only seen ice in a martini, you know."

She shuddered again and bit her lip in irritation. Hal Bailey was the last person to whom she ever wanted to show any weakness.

Billy mumbled something.

"What was that?" Hal tossed Billy an irritable look. He kept massaging Jen's wrist with a surprising gentleness.

Billy looked straight ahead at the darkness falling over the flat land. "She's strong. But if she's starting to get the shakes, you should hold her. Hey... she's not bad—you shouldn't mind holding her."

Billy paused and regarded Hal's crackling glare. The boy went on quickly, "Don't blame me—I'm telling the truth and you know it."

Jen blushed, which she rarely did. And, cursing her unreliable body, she felt another shiver ripple through her. She'd gotten so cold on the ice that she wasn't sure she'd ever be warm again.

Hal kept a firm hold on her wrist but made no other move toward her. He looked disgusted with her, Billy and the world in general. Still, Jen knew that she had done better on the ice than he ever would have expected. He might not like to admit it, but she had.

"Could you really just let the whales die?" Jen asked, breaking the awkward silence between them. "If the weather doesn't open a way out for them?"

His hand was hot against her cold wrist. "If the weather gets worse, it may be kinder not to let them suffer."

"Look," he said, watching her downcast and disapproving face, "nature plays for keeps up here." His grip on her wrist tightened—he wanted her to understand that he was not cruel, only realistic. "The Arctic notices every mistake," he said. "If the whales don't start south in time, they die. That's how nature works. It weeds out the weak, the stupid, those whose instincts don't function correctly."

"What about the innocent?" She turned from him to stare out at the falling darkness.

"What about them?"

"Does nature kill the innocent, too? What good does that do?"

"Innocence has nothing to do with it."

"Somebody ought to help them," she insisted.

"We've done everything we can. Everything. If we could get them to move to a different hole we could lead them to the sea. We can't. We've tried everything. All we can do now is hope the weather breaks."

"And if it doesn't?"

"We do the best we can."

Wordlessly she pried his fingers off her wrist. She pulled her hand away and rubbed it gingerly, as if to scrub off the memory of his touch. She knew Keenan would say the same thing exactly, but somehow she expected Hal Bailey to be able to do more. "You don't have much sympathy do you?"

His voice was as bitter as hers. "The whales should have read the signs. They should have stayed with their own kind, gone where they belonged. This isn't the place for them."

Jen bit her lip. "Like me?" she asked. "They should have headed back for California. They weren't made for a place like this." *They're not smart enough or tough enough or good enough,* she thought.

He turned from her. He stared straight ahead. Only thickening darkness greeted his gaze. "Exactly," he said wearily. "Exactly like you."

BACK AT A.R.F. Hal told Billy to put the truck back in the motor pool and unload it. He tried to take Jen's arm when she got out of the Jeep, but she shook off his hand. He opened the door that led to her living quarters, and she breezed past him, saying nothing.

He followed her down the short hallway, watched as she fumbled with her key. Her fingers were still stiff and awkward from the cold. He took the key from her, unlocked the door with a single precise twist.

"I've had a phone put back in for you. So you can call your grandfather," he said. "I'll wait while you change. Take a shower, that's the best way to warm up. Then I'll take you for something to eat."

She entered the room with the grateful feeling of one coming home. Last night it had looked bleak to her. This evening it looked like a paradise of warmth and luxury. The phone sat like a precious black jewel on the bedside table. A line to the outside world. She wanted nothing more than to be alone in this marvelous room, to try to phone in her story.

"I'm not hungry." She tried to shut the door behind her.

He held it open. "You've got to eat. Do you know how much energy you burned today?"

"I'm not hungry." She pushed at the door. His strength made it impossible to budge.

He tilted his head and gave her a suspicious look. "Are you afraid everybody's heard about Keenan by now? That he's married? You don't have to be embarrassed. I'll escort you in, help smooth things over."

"You? Ha!" She met his blue eyes contemptuously. "Asking you to smooth things over would be like asking Attila the Hun to be a peacemaker."

"Listen—" A dangerous expression crossed his face.

"You listen," she ordered. "I've got phone calls to make. Go eat by yourself. I've been the spectacle of the dining hall once today. If you talk to Keenan and Helena, give them my congratulations. I'll send them a present as soon as I'm somewhere I can shop." She tried once more to shut the door. Once more his grasp kept it immovable.

His gloves were off, and she saw how his knuckles whitened. "You're stubborn."

"You're right." She hoped there was danger in her own stance. He was a hard, cold, overbearing man, and she'd had enough of him for a lifetime.

He stared at her. She stared back. At last he gave a hopeless sideways glance as if looking for some sense in the situation. "All right. Stay here. But get in the shower, dammit, and warm up."

"Fine. Go away and let me."

He set his mouth and pulled the door shut. She stood staring after him, breathing hard. Her knees felt weak. From the look he had given her, he would gladly leave her alone to starve. That was fine. She was exhausted by the emotional turmoil he always stirred within her.

She shuffled out of her cap, gloves, parka, sweater, slacks, and underwear. She took a long, tingling shower until she felt her blood circulating with its usual vigor. She slipped into her nightgown and was tying the belt on her blue robe when her phone rang.

She looked at it for a moment, as if it were something that had just sprung into supernatural life. Who could it be? she wondered nervously. Keenan? Hal?

With trepidation she lifted the receiver. "Yes?"

"Where the devil have you been?" her grandfather's voice demanded. "I've been trying all day to get you. What's this unspeakable nonsense about Keenan being married? Get home. I won't have you near the idiot."

Dagobert's voice sounded fuzzy, as if it came from another planet.

"He's got a right to his own life." Jen's tone was crisp. "Now maybe you'll leave him alone. *And* me."

"He's broken Ferd's heart," Dagobert stormed. "He's broken a poor old man's heart. He might as well have driven a dagger through him."

Ferd Brubecker, Jen reflected sardonically, had approximately the same sensibilities as a shark and was about as likely to have his heart broken. What Dagobert meant was that Ferd was hopping mad.

"As for me," Dagobert continued, "I've always treated that boy like a son. This is how he repays me. By jilting my granddaughter. I ought to shake him till his teeth rattle, the insolent pup."

"He's not a boy. He's thirty years old. He didn't jilt me. There was nothing between us."

"He's jilted you for some—some Eskimo maiden," Dagobert said in disgust. "He's lost his grasp. He's gone native. The cold must have numbed his brain."

"He didn't jilt me," Jen protested, her patience failing. "What difference if he marries an Eskimo woman? I hear she's extremely nice. I'm sure he—he just thought that eloping was the best way to put an end to all the manipulation."

"Get home," Dagobert ordered. "I don't want you near him. I intend to have your name in every society column on the west coast, and Ferd will, by God, help me. I'm arranging a date for you with that prince—

what's his name?—the one who isn't married yet. He's going to be in California soon. And one of those Massachusetts boys will be in town. You can go out with him, too. He's a president's nephew. Come to think of it, why should you settle for a president's nephew? I'll see that a president's son has you on his arm. Nobody's going to treat my granddaughter like—"

"I don't want to go out with a prince," Jen said hotly. "I don't want to go out with a president's nephew, a president's son, or the president himself—"

"And what's more, I'm getting you a different job," Dagobert fumed. "Ferd and I agree. He's letting you go. It's ridiculous to have you working on wedding news. It's salt in the wound. Break with journalism altogether. It's no field for a woman—too cynical."

"You and Ferd can't fire me," Jen said in disbelief. "I told you—I wasn't coming back there after this. I'm going to find another job—on another newspaper."

"Pah!" sputtered her grandfather. "It's time to stop playing games. Get home."

"I'm onto a story right now," she told him, more in retaliation than conviction.

"Story?" He laughed. "Up there? What could happen up there? Who's even there? A bunch of polar bears?"

"There's a very dramatic story here, for your information. Two California gray whales are trapped in the ice."

Dagobert snorted. "Who cares? A couple of fat fish get stuck in the ice? Ridiculous. Ah, come home, Jen. I miss you."

Jen gripped the phone more tightly. "I'm sorry. No."

"The cretin Keenan had the gall to phone me this afternoon. He said this wasn't your fault. It was his. I said,

'You most certainly have that correct, you pea brain.' And I told him if he was half a man, he'd have you on a plane home to me without further ado."

"Keenan doesn't take orders from you. Neither do I. I'm not coming home."

"Of course you are. The moron married somebody else. There's no reason for you to be there. Get home. Now. Be a good girl and I'll have a prince on your doorstep, just like you were Cinderella."

Jen knew it was useless to argue. "I don't want to talk about it. I'm hanging up."

"Young lady, if you hang up on me, you'll have to come begging to me on your hands and knees. You will not hang up on me."

"I'm hanging up, and I'm not going to beg you for anything. I told you once—I'm on my own. I won't ask you for anything. If I ever do, then fine. Then I'll do whatever you want. But in the meantime I'm living my own life."

"You're as big a ninny as Keenan. Be home tomorrow night. You belong at your granddaddy's side." And to prove he was still in charge, he hung up on her as loudly as possible.

Jen sat down on the edge of her bed. For a moment she chewed at the inside of her cheek with frustration. She wanted nothing more than to show Dagobert she could succeed without him. She had a story, all right, but no one to give it to. She thought hard for a moment. Maybe she could show Ferd Brubecker—and his whole chain of papers, as well.

She reached for the phone and dialed the paper where, for eleven long and fruitless months, she had worked for Ferd Brubecker. They knew her there—she'd surprise them with the magnitude of the story she'd found.

She identified herself and asked to talk to Bill Lazlow, the night editor. She didn't know Lazlow well, and he seemed nervous as soon as he heard her name. "I'm sorry you won't be with us any longer," he said. "Mr. Brubecker announced you'll be leaving us. I'm—uh—sorry about—uh—everything, Miss Martinson."

"Lazlow," she said desperately, "I think I've got a story up here. I'm through with the society page—but this is big. Will you take the facts and give them to somebody for a rewrite?"

After some cajoling, Lazlow, sounding more dubious than before, agreed. Jen set her teeth in determination, closed her eyes and marshaled the information—she told him all about the trapped whales.

"That's all?" Lazlow asked, disappointed.

"I could give you a lot more details. I have pictures. I could send them on the next plane."

Lazlow said she could send the pictures if she wanted, but that it wasn't much of a story. Maybe he'd file it; he didn't know; it didn't seem worth much.

"Never mind," Jen said. "I tried to do you a favor. Forget it. And for your information, Mr. Brubecker can't fire me because I told him via my grandfather that I was quitting. This makes it official—I *quit*."

Jen hung up, her frustration greater than before. She dialed information and asked for the phone numbers of the papers in Anchorage and Fairbanks. She called, identifying herself as a free-lance reporter from San Francisco. She told herself it wasn't a lie. She was a reporter, she was from San Francisco, and she was now as free-lance as she could possibly get.

The man at the desk in Fairbanks seemed more interested in finding out why a woman from San Francisco was in Ultima than about the trapped whales. The woman at the desk in Anchorage was curter, more businesslike. She acted as if the story was, possibly, of some interest.

Jen hung up and sat feeling dejected. Was this it? she wondered. Could she interest nobody in the two whales? Was Hal, hard-hearted as he was, right, after all?

She looked at her camera bag on the dresser. She took out the tape recorder and rewound the tape. She was surprised that the machine worked after being in the punishing cold, but it did, perfectly.

There, in the snug safety of her room, she heard the haunting noise again: the slow, desperate breathing of two giants faced with death. In her mind's eye, she saw Hal reaching out his hand and the whale accepting his caress.

Rewinding the tape, she shook her head in consternation. Dagobert said nobody would care about the whales. Hal had said the same thing. And what if people did care? What good would it do? She didn't even know. She would simply try to see.

She smoothed back her hair and tossed her braid out of the way, so that it hung over her back. She dialed information again and asked for the number of a radio station she'd listened to when she was in college: radio KXXO. In the evenings it ran a telephone call-in show, sometimes informative, sometimes silly, sometimes controversial. The host would listen to her because he would listen to anybody.

She waited while the phone rang a seemingly eternal number of times. At last it was answered by a station operator who asked her to hold. Then she heard a man with a professionally cheerful voice.

"Good evening, you're on the air. This is *San Francisco Speaks*, and I'm Long John Silverburg, your host.

Tonight's question is Flying Saucer Abductions—Do They Really Happen? What's your name, and have you ever, heh-heh, been abducted by a flying saucer?"

Drat, Jen thought, Long John Silverburg had set off in one of his more exotic directions. "My name is Jennifer Martinson," she said carefully. "I'm a free-lance reporter, and I'm calling from the Arctic Research Facility near Ultima, Alaska—"

"Wow," said Long John Silverburg in his rich, syrupy voice. "Those space aliens really took you for a ride, didn't they, darling?"

It took Jennifer almost two full minutes to convince him that she was neither eccentric nor joking and that there really were two whales trapped in the Arctic ice.

"Hey, hey, hey, Sugar, you sound *serious*," he said at last. "You're really in Alaska? Is that why you sound so far away?"

"I'm deadly serious," Jen answered. "I saw these whales myself. I have photographs. There's almost two miles of ice between them and a way to the open sea. I've got a recording of them breathing."

"You're talking about gray whales? You're talking about California's official state marine mammal?" His voice had the uniquely smarmy brand of sincerity peculiar to radio voices.

"I am. And this is what they sound like." Jen switched on the tape. Between the pauses in the whale's long, sighing breaths, she explained the situation in greater detail.

"That sounds pathetic, sweetheart," Long John said. "Let's hear that tape again."

Jen replayed the tape.

"This is outrageous," Long John said. "They're actually thinking of killing these animals? Who did you say was in charge up there?"

"Bailey. Dr. Hal Bailey."

"San Francisco, are you listening? Dr. Hal Bailey wants to kill the whales. *Our* whales."

"I didn't say he *wanted* to kill them," Jen interjected guiltily. But she objected in vain. Long John Silverburg had discovered a topic more juicy than space aliens. When she finally hung up, she had an eerie feeling that she had gotten her story to the public, but not quite the way she had wanted to.

A knock shattered the silence of the little room. She sprang to her feet and opened the door.

"Room service," Hal said sardonically, entering uninvited. He carried a tray which he set on the bedside table. "I talked to Keenan and Helena. They send you their regards. I also brought you the rarest item in Ultima. A drink."

He pulled a silver flask from his pocket and got two glasses from the little bathroom. He poured a finger of brandy into each. He handed one of the tumblers to her. "Cheers," he said and tossed down the liquor in one gulp.

Jen sat down on the edge of the bed and lifted the towel that covered the tray. She didn't want to admit it, but she was starving. To see a plate of spaghetti and meatballs seemed amazing. To see a fresh salad, crisp and green, was nothing short of a wonder.

"I'm not hungry," she lied, and immediately started eating.

"So I see." He crossed his arms and watched her attack the food.

"This morning food was only food," she said, slathering butter on a dinner roll. "Tonight it seems like a miracle."

"It is a miracle." He sat down in the room's single chair. "Everything humans can do up here is a miracle."

"How did Billy's people do it?" she asked, savoring her coffee. "How did they endure up here for 5,000 years?"

"The biggest miracle of all. But in the last hundred years, we've nearly obliterated what it took them 5,000 years to perfect. We've killed most of the whales, tampered with the ecology, run the fool pipeline through the country and changed the economy forever."

"My grandfather was one of the people who had that pipeline built," she said uneasily. "I suppose you blame him for everything." Dagobert still held an interest in MaLaBar, the company that owned and used the pipeline.

"I just stated facts." His steady gaze was not one of admiration.

"Is that one more reason for you not to like me?"

"I'd like you fine if you were in California where you belong."

"I don't belong in California any longer. I'm on my own now. I'm making my own way."

"Should I have Keenan call, try to talk some sense into you?"

"Keenan should attend to his wife," Jen said with asperity. "I will *not* be pushed around by my grandfather. Or anybody else."

"Keenan says your grandfather is a meddling old coot. He wants to run everybody's life."

"He is. He does. But you don't have any right to talk about him. So don't." She finished her spaghetti and began on the chocolate cake.

"Drink your brandy. I don't know why I wasted it on you. You seem to have recovered all right."

"I'm the recovering type."

"You're the sassy type."

"With you, I don't have much choice. Are you going back out on the ice tomorrow? To see the whales? I'm going with you."

He cocked a brown eyebrow in disapproval. "The devil you are."

Jen picked up her glass of brandy. "Try to stop me." She held the tumbler toward him as if in a toast. "I'll walk there if I have to." She downed the brandy as neatly as he had. "Skoal," she said, although her throat burned.

He shook his head in disgust. "You'd do it, wouldn't you?"

"Yes. And I'm glad you realize it."

"Then I hope you enjoy the walk."

"I hope you enjoy letting me walk. I consider you a lout, you know."

The phone rang. Jen jumped, clutching her robe more tightly around her. She hoped it wasn't her grandfather again.

She was startled to hear a stranger's voice. "Is Hal there?"

Jen's cheeks flamed with nervous energy. "It's for you," she said and thrust the receiver at Hal.

She would have flounced out of the room but there was nowhere appropriate to flounce. Her grandfather had exasperated her, the media had frustrated her, and now

Hal had stretched her tolerance to its limit. He seemed incapable of speaking two civil sentences in a row to her.

Crossing her arms, she cast a resentful glance at him. He looked almost frighteningly serious as he listened to the voice on the other end of the phone. "Yes?" he kept saying. "Yes?" He shook his head, registering half anger, half distaste. "Don't say anything. I'll be there in a minute," he said at last.

He hung up the phone and glowered at her. "What's wrong?" she asked sweetly. "Does some walrus somewhere have the mumps?"

She stood between the bed and the dresser. He took a step toward her, his face grim.

"That was Kelpington, our meteorologist. He says we've just had eleven calls. For me. Protesting that I shouldn't kill those whales. Calls from San Francisco. One mentioned you."

"Oh," Jen said lamely.

"He also said the *Anchorage Daily News* called to confirm that the whales are trapped."

"Oh." Suddenly the room seemed too hot to her, too closed in and too small. If she were not almost as tall as Hal, she would have sworn he was towering over her.

"He says the phone in the central office's been ringing for the last ten minutes. You did this, didn't you? I don't know how, or how you did it so fast, but *you* made it happen. Didn't you?"

She winced at his tone. She nodded and looked at the floor. He took another step toward her.

He reached out and took her braid in his hand. She felt the heat of his fist next to the nape of her neck. He forced her face up, to look into his. "Witch," he said between his teeth. "That's what you are. A beautiful blond young witch."

He did something that surprised him as much as it did her. It was neither reasonable nor scientific. He kissed her.

CHAPTER SIX

"WITCH," HE REPEATED against her lips, then kissed her again. With one hand he clasped the back of her neck, and his other arm circled her waist tightly.

His lips moved against hers with sureness, heat and hunger. Anger, too, was in the kiss, as if he didn't wish to touch her, but was compelled to by a force stronger than will.

Jen, who had called him a "lout" only moments before, found herself winding her arms around his neck. He seemed as warm and strong as a flame of pure life. A strange fluttering filled her chest, ran down her body in ripples, making her thighs feel weak and her knees tremble. She was staggered to realize she had never felt desire before she had met Hal Bailey. Now she felt it so powerfully that it frightened her.

He drew back slightly. Once again he took her braid in his hand. Running his thumb over the blue ribbon that tied it, he held the tip just beneath her chin, as if he would tickle her. "I keep wondering what it'd be like to undo this," he breathed. "Wondering what you'd look like with it loose. What it'd be like to run my hands through it. To see it falling over your naked shoulders."

She took an uneven breath and stared into his eyes. They were bluer than the flawless Arctic sky had been and so intent they robbed her of words. All she could do was cling to him, her pulses running in sweet riot.

"You can't be Brubecker's blonde." He dropped the braid and took her chin between his fingers. "Not if you can kiss another man like that. He misread the signals. You never loved him, did you?"

"No." Her voice was strained. "I told you that." She wasn't sure what would happen next or what she wanted to happen. She had always valued her freedom, had been careful not to give away her heart. Now both her heart and body ached with unwise yearnings.

"I shouldn't be holding you." He frowned but didn't release her. "You know that."

She nodded, the blood tingling in her cheeks. "I know."

"And you shouldn't be holding me."

"I know that, too." She could feel the vein in her throat pounding wildly and knew that he, too, must feel it, throbbing beneath his touch.

"You know this is only biology, don't you? It doesn't mean anything. It doesn't mean we're in love. All it can do is cause trouble."

The words wounded her. He might feel an unwanted flicker of desire for her, but he didn't like her. Their bodies might speak to each other; their hearts and minds could not.

"You have two reasons to go home now," he said. "To get out of Keenan's life. And to get out of mine. Whatever happens between you and me can't end well."

He exhaled harshly and moved his hands up to disengage hers from around his neck. But his body remained close to hers as if some powerful magnetism held him. He picked up the golden weight of her braid again. "I want to undo this." He gave her his rare smile. It was cynical, but it made her heart waver and struggle to maintain its balance. "Don't ever let me."

He pulled the ribbon off. He handed it to her, then let the hair fall from his grasp. She looked at him with a kind of desperate boldness. "Why shouldn't I? I'm an adult."

He took a step away. He shook his head. Once again she saw that glimmer of something in his eyes that wasn't tame and wasn't safe. "You're a kid. A rich kid with a lot to learn. You're a Martinson. A woman born to complicate things. I like life simple."

Hurt, she straightened her back and stood taller. She'd show him she was a Martinson, all right. "Then why don't you simplify your life right now... and get out of my room?"

"Right." His voice resonated with irony. "I've got to go—and straighten up whatever mess you've made this time."

"Good luck. Just hope I can't make trouble faster than you can straighten it out."

He gave her a scathing look that ended up resting on her lips. "That's exactly what I'm hoping. You're heedless, Jen. Heedless women are dangerous."

He didn't smile again, he simply left. When he closed the door, Jen threw herself on the bed and hugged the hard pillow. She tried to bury her hot face in it.

She knew, to her humiliation, that all he felt for her was a renegade lust, fierce but meaningless. He felt no affection or respect. He never would, because she was a Martinson. Although he had awakened something in her no other man had ever touched, she knew he was more dangerous to her than the dark, forbidding land of the Arctic.

He was wrong about her; she wasn't heedless, she told herself fervently. She had simply been caught up in a series of events in which each was more unpredictable than the last.

She was certain she had begun by doing the right thing. She had defied her grandfather and Ferd, and she had agreed to talk to Keenan only so that the two of them could present a united front to the two old meddlers. But from that point on, things kept falling into greater and greater chaos.

The phone rang again and she sat up, smoothing her hair. Her cheeks still burned. Who was calling now? Her grandfather again? Hal to tell her to pack up and leave—no further arguments? Keenan to try to convince her to go home, just as her grandfather and Hal wanted?

She lifted the receiver and heard a stranger's voice. The man identified himself as Walter F. Stonebridger, editor of the *Sentinel* of Redwood City, California. He had heard her and the tapes of the whales on Long John's show.

"You said you have photos? Have you sent them to anybody?"

"No." Jen was nervous, unsure what the man wanted.

"Send them to me," Stonebridger said. "Immediately. Tell me this story about the whales again. In detail. I'll see you get a byline. And a regular salary while you cover this for us. You're free-lance, right? You're interested in this proposition?"

"Yes." Her voice had gone shaky with excitement. "On both counts." The Redwood *Sentinel* was a small paper, one Ferd Brubecker had never bothered to acquire. He considered it radical and irresponsible, a paper so bad it made his look excellent by comparison. Jen rather liked it, except that, at least twice a year, claws bared, it went after her grandfather. It didn't like the Martinson Corporation, the oil company's environmental policies, or Dagobert himself.

"This is ironic." Stonebridger had a gravelly voice, as if he'd spent a lifetime smoking cigarettes. "On the radio you said you're Dagobert Martinson's granddaughter. I've clashed with Dagobert. Are you sure you want to work for me?"

"I've clashed with Dagobert myself. I want to work, period."

"I thought you worked for the Brubecker paper in San Francisco. I heard you were engaged to one of the Brubecker heirs. But that he just married someone else. Is that why you're willing to work for us?"

Jen's mind spun. Perhaps the man was more interested in gossip about her and Keenan than news about the whales. "I no longer work for the Brubeckers. I was never engaged to Keenan Brubecker. I wish him happiness. Look, Mr. Stonebridger, if you want to hear about whales, ask. That's the only story I'm interested in telling."

To her surprise, he laughed. "You've got a sexy voice, sweetheart, but when you talk like that, I hear old Dagobert in you. Tough, are you?"

"No," she answered. "Trying to learn, that's all."

"Okay, Martinson, tell me about your whales."

Good heavens, Jen thought in dizzy wonder, *I've got a job.* As completely and carefully as she could, she began to explain once more about the trapped whales.

AN ABRUPT KNOCK on her door woke Jen at six in the morning. She tried to bury her head under the pillow, but the knocking continued. She instinctively knew only one man could knock with such infuriating loudness and persistence: Hal Bailey. Had he thought of a new way to torment her and couldn't wait until a decent hour to test it?

The heat in her room had forced her to strip off her nightgown before she could sleep. She reached for her robe, pulled it around her and staggered to the door.

"Get dressed. Come on," Hal said without ceremony. He wore low-slung jeans and a camel-colored sweater.

"Go away," she yawned. "It's still dark out."

"It's dark till ten in the morning. Get dressed. We're having breakfast in my apartment."

"Who's 'we'? I don't want to eat in your apartment. I don't want to eat with you."

"Get dressed or I'll dress you myself," he practically snapped. "I have a problem—that you created. We need to talk where it's private."

Jen yawned and stretched. She forgot she had nothing on under her robe, and her motions gave Hal an excellent glimpse of her cleavage. His face was impassive, but she saw a disturbing glint flash deep in his eyes. It brought her quickly awake. After last night she wasn't sure she wanted to be alone with him again.

He put his hands on her shoulders and turned her around, propelling her toward the closet. "Dress," he repeated. "I also want to try to talk some sense into you—make you go home. Where you belong."

She remembered her new job for the Redwood City *Sentinel. I have a few surprises for you. And for Dagobert, too,* she thought with satisfaction.

Sweeping clean clothes and lingerie into her arms, she strode into the bathroom. Quickly she dressed in her warmest clothes, black wool slacks and a heather-colored sweater. When she rejoined Hal, she said nothing to him and he said nothing to her.

Wordlessly they left the room, and wordlessly he led her to another part of the facility's compound. They might have been strangers, sharing the same hallways for a few moments.

She felt a flutter of apprehension as Hal paused before a door in another anonymous-looking hallway. This was where he lived, she thought with an odd feeling. She wondered what sort of "problem" he had spoken of, and a frisson of foreboding surged through her.

Hal's apartment, although small, was not stark and cold as she had imagined it. The walls had been paneled in oak. A well-worn Persian carpet covered the tiles; the oak and glass-topped coffee table was strewn with magazines and books. The scents of coffee and bacon filled the air.

A television and VCR stood next to a compact disc player with a collection of discs shelved next to it. Semi-classical music played in the background, a light tinkling of piano notes. A leafy vine grew in one brass pot and a fat cactus in another.

Hal gestured toward a small dining area. "I had Arnold get up early and send over breakfast. Sit." It was more order than invitation.

She glanced warily at the oak table set with gleaming chafing dishes, sensible china and silvery coffee service. Hal pulled out her chair for her, a gesture of politeness that startled her. She sat and so did he. The two of them stared at each other as if some kind of time bomb lay between them, ticking away.

"Coffee?" He began to fill her cup before she had time to answer.

"Thanks."

Without asking he began heaping food on both their plates even though she had no appetite. Silence hung, weighted, between them.

"Listen," he said at last, his voice brusque. "We had over twenty calls from California last night. Raising hell over those whales. The phone's already ringing in the central office. What I want to know—" he allowed his displeased gaze to settle on Jen "—is what you did to bring this on."

She shifted warily. "I called some newspapers. And a radio station in San Francisco. The Long John Silverburg show."

Hal gave her a general all-purpose glower. "Silverburg? The guy's always making the newspapers. His life's one long publicity stunt."

"Well, at least he listened," Jen said in her own defense. "Nobody else seemed to want to."

"Silverburg's the worst lunatic in radio. He'll do anything for attention. No wonder this got blown out of proportion. People will think we're after Bambi with machine guns."

"I only told the truth," Jen protested, putting down her fork. She could not force herself to eat the eggs and bacon set before her. "I only said that the whales were trapped and that if they couldn't be freed, there was talk of—well, killing them."

"*You* talked of *me* killing them. Half of those calls personally threatened *me*. One little kid called up bawling, begging me not to—hysterical. Then her mother got on the phone and said *I* ought to be harpooned."

Jen crumpled her napkin in her lap and stared down at it, rebelliously refusing to meet his gaze.

"I want a retraction," Hal told her. "On behalf of this entire facility. I want it immediately."

A retraction? She could make no retraction. She had said nothing untrue. She had merely given Long John the facts. Although Hal's anger unsettled her, she refused to wilt before its force. She drew herself up and looked him in the eye. "No," she said.

"What?"

She forced herself to keep her expression calm, her look level. "Those whales *are* trapped. You did say they might have to be destroyed. I refuse to retract the truth."

He set his teeth. "Calling some weirdo radio show was irresponsible."

Her heart hammered, but she refused to retreat. "My job is to release news. That's what I did."

"You had no business—"

Jen, her blood running high now, cut him off. "I had no business doing my job? That makes no sense. Nobody thinks I'm serious. Well, I got my story out. Maybe it was only over Long John Silverburg's show, but I got it to the public. It made an impact. People are concerned about those whales."

"Fine," Hal said out of the corner of his mouth. "You've proved your point. Now tell Long John What's-his-face I'm not a mad-dog killer. Then go back to California. To your grandfather. Where you belong."

His displeased gaze burned into her like a laser beam. She didn't flinch. "My job is with the story. The Redwood City *Sentinel* called last night. They hired me."

An expression of surprise crossed his face. "The Redwood City *Sentinel*? The liberal little paper that's always on the warpath? The one that hates people like your grandfather? What are you up to now?"

"I have to work for somebody. I don't work for Keenan's family anymore. I quit—I'm not taking special favors from anybody, Dagobert included. I'll make my own way."

He took a deep breath. The woman was shaking his tidy existence into disorder. He needed to get out the heavy artillery and drive her off. He set down his coffee cup with an emphatic *thump*. "You've already sensationalized the whole mess enough. No more. Go back to your grandfather and make everybody happy. He promises to go on spoiling you in the style to which you're accustomed."

This time Jen did flinch. He didn't want her at the facility nor did anyone else. The only person anywhere who wanted her for any reason was Dagobert. Then a spark of suspicion flickered within her. "What do you mean—my grandfather promises? What do you know about him?"

Hal's face was stony. "He called. In fact, he offered me ten thousand dollars to have you on the next plane to California. I'd love to see you on it. I'd drive you to the airport myself."

The blood surged to her cheeks. She was humiliated and infuriated. Worse, she was deeply disappointed in Hal, who was now in league with Dagobert, of all people. "You hypocrite."

Hal sighed. All he wanted was to be free of this woman and the thousand temptations she offered. She offered more than she could ever know. She offered so many that his head hurt.

He pushed his chair back from the table, his jaw set. "I told him what to do with his lousy money. I don't need it. And I won't do his baby-sitting for him. But I will try to reason with you. You belong with him. You have a good life back there. Go to it."

Open-mouthed, Jen stared at him. "You just want me off the story. That's why you're doing this. You're actually trying to help *him*."

"I'm not doing anything for him. I hung up on him. But before I did he said to tell you this—if you come home he'll find you a new job and he'll never mention Keenan—or Alaska—again. Your life will be smooth as silk. He says he'll give you anything you want. Anything. Think about it."

Jen stared at him, her lips still parted in amazement. His face was as cold as the ice outside; his eyes were slitted in a speculative gaze as if he could see right through her. He was watching her as a hunter might watch prey. Did he really think she cared more about comforts and luxury than her freedom, her very integrity?

"You hypocrite," she repeated, contempt in her voice.

His eyes narrowed even more. A blue vein in his temple throbbed. No other part of his body moved. He seemed poised, marking time.

The hurt stabbed more deeply within her, and she struck out at Hal because he had inflicted it. "Don't you get tired of carrying rich men's messages? Or does it make you feel important?"

She knew her jibe struck the mark. Something glittered deep within his steady gaze. The silence in the room swelled dangerously. The vein at his temple leaped again, but the rest of his face stayed immobile.

Jen's face, in contrast, was a study in emotions. Her chin was stubborn, her mouth rebellious, and her cheeks so pink they burned. "Sit there like a statue of the abominable snowman if you want," she said between her teeth, "but it's true. Keenan's too sweet—and too wimpy—to tell me he's marrying somebody else. So who rushes to tell me for him? Good old Hal Bailey." She shook her head in disdain. "My grandfather wants me to know that if I just behave, life will be 'smooth as silk'—" she made an impatient gesture "—and who comes scurrying out of the woodwork to carry the news? Good old Hal Bailey, the rich man's friend."

The room became so quiet that she thought she could hear the pounding of her pulses. Not even a clock ticked. At last Hal spoke, his tone sinisterly even. "I wouldn't talk like that."

"I'll talk anyway I want. According to you, my grandfather's beneath contempt. But you're pleading his case for him. I'm sure he'd like that. Why don't you get down on your knees for him? I'm sure he'd like that even more."

He gave a long, slow exhalation. Then he sat simply staring at her.

She pushed away from the table. "You act as if he can't buy you, but that he can buy me. Or maybe he can't buy you because he didn't offer a high enough price. It hardly matters. You're doing what he wants anyway."

She rose to her feet so fast it almost made her dizzy. She wanted out of his rooms. The walls seemed to close in on her, choking the breath out of her. Hal was on his feet almost as swiftly as she.

She headed for the door, but he blocked her exit. When she tried to forge past him, he put out his hands to take her by the arms and hold her in place. Jen sprang backward at his touch. She didn't want to be near him. She stood, backed against the table, staring at him and breathing hard. Her heartbeat drummed in her ears.

He looked furious. He had her cornered, and this time she couldn't move away when he seized her. "All I want is to restore some order up here. I don't like your grandfather. But one thing's clear—he loves you. His morals may be lousy, and he may be a manipulative old geezer, but his emotion runs deep. When a man loves something that much—" He stopped suddenly, his fingers tightening on her shoulders.

Jen squared her shoulders, trying not to shiver at his touch. The word *love* coming from his lips jarred her. So did the intensity of his expression. She gave him a searching look. "When a man loves something that much? Then what?"

He exhaled sharply. For a dizzying second she thought he was going to pull her closer, kiss her again. He released her instead. "Go to him. What do you care about these whales—really?"

Jen's temples pounded. She was so filled with fervent emotions that she trembled. "I care about them because they're alive and in trouble. They're fellow creatures. Don't be self-righteous. I'm not the one that wants to kill them—"

His face darkened. "I don't want to kill anything. I'd like to save them—they don't belong here any more than you do."

He reached out again to grip her shoulder for emphasis. She struck his hands away. She saw the glint in his eye and managed to slip away from his nearness, to take refuge on the other side of the table. He flexed his fingers, fighting the impulse to go after her, to force her to listen and obey, for once in her life.

"I'm staying until the story ends, one way or the other," she said as evenly as she could. "You won't stop me."

His mouth became a bitter line. He said nothing. She could feel displeasure radiating from him, but she pretended it didn't affect her. "So...what time are we going to see the whales?" she asked, sounding almost flippant. "And by the way, can you have somebody take some film into Ultima and have it flown to Anchorage?"

There was a long and pregnant silence. His mouth went a fraction more crooked, a shade more bitter.

"I suppose I can just put it in the mail drop by the dining hall," she mused. "And by the way, I'm not going to retract anything. I suggest you prepare some kind of statement for anybody who calls objecting about you sending those whales to whale heaven."

Inwardly he cursed the fates that had brought him, the whales and this woman together. "I'm *not* sending them to whale heaven."

"Oh?" she asked, her eyes wide with innocence. "You're going to save them?"

His expression grew harder. "It's impossible to get them to move. Only the weather can save them. You know it as well as I do."

"Oh?" she asked with the same naïveté. "Then you'll stand around and watch them die. That doesn't sound good, either. I'd work on a statement. An extremely good one. You'll need it."

"Damn! Don't make me the villain."

"I don't intend to. I only intend to report the facts. So I'd like your cooperation. I want to go out on the ice today."

"No. I only took you yesterday to keep an eye on you."

"You also thought I might find myself a little story. Well, I did. I'd hate to report now that you're blocking news coverage."

Hal leaned across the table and thrust a finger in her face. "I'll take you on the ice, all right. You can stay out there until you're begging to come back here. You want to cover news? All right—cover it. If you freeze your ears off, don't blame me."

"Fine," she said, her chin high. "I'll meet you in your office in ten minutes."

I stood up to my grandfather, and I'll stand up to you, she thought. *You're strong, but so am I. And I'm going to show you that I'm not what you think.*

Head high, she swept past him and into the living room. She was out the door and walking swiftly back to her own room. There, alone in the winding corridor, her brief sense of resolve melted away. For a moment she had forgotten the most important thing—the whales. The whales, she thought...how oddly her fate had become entwined with theirs. And how odd that her story had created such an unexpected impact.

Suddenly, for no reason, she was frightened. It was as if a ghostly breeze blew through the hallway. An unearthly feeling gripped her, chilling her through.

She had an eerie premonition that everything hung poised, waiting. The sensation was so strong that she stopped, looking around her uneasily. Something was about to happen, something big. When it did, she sensed it would shake apart the tidy world she knew.

She could feel a strange force rising like a storm wind. Yes, somehow, everything was going to change. Something was going to happen. Soon.

CHAPTER SEVEN

JEN STOOD on the ice, remembering her strange moment of presentiment. She looked around her. In spite of that intimation of change, nothing at all had changed, she thought in despair. Nothing.

The landscape still looked like some cold lunar plain. The sea was frozen just as solid as before. The sky was just as blue, flawless, and hard as it had been yesterday. And the two whales were still trapped.

The ice had not shifted, the lead to the open sea had not cracked its way any nearer. No new lead had appeared, breaking the white barrier. No new breathing hole had yawned open. No wind stirred to augur any change.

Jen had ridden to the site with a silent Hal and a cheerful Billy Owen. Now, while the two men tried to adjust some mysterious part of the video camera, she stood at the edge of the breathing hole, looking out through the white fur of her parka hood. Her argument with Hal had left her feeling empty and sick.

"It's the same," she said tonelessly. She'd hoped that today the sun would rise up, huge and powerful, melting a path to the safety of the open sea. But it hadn't. It shone dimly, a faint disk that seemed to warm nothing.

Billy was busy swearing under his breath at the camera. He swore in two languages, which took most of his concentration.

She was startled when Hal spoke. "It's not the same. It's worse."

She studied his face, to see if he was joking. Like Billy, he seemed impervious to the cold. He didn't even bother to put up the hood of his parka. His hair fell over his eyes, and his breath billowed up in a crystalline plume.

"It's not worse. It's exactly the same," Jen said.

Eyes narrowed, Hal glanced at the sky. "It's worse. The temperature's falling. More ice is forming. We're getting a pressure ridge developing between here and the open water. If it grows, it'll be like a wall between the whales and open water. And the whales aren't just more scraped up. They're weaker."

His words fell on her heart like stones. The weather was growing worse, and a few degrees meant the difference between life and death.

Jen turned from Hal, not liking the implacability of his face. He could be as cruel and matter-of-fact as nature itself. Billy, having subdued the video camera and surrendered it to Hal, strolled to her side. He nodded down at the ice. "See how it looks like an oily film?"

She nodded.

"That's Frazil ice. When it gets thicker, then crystals start to form. Then we start getting real ice—we call it shorefast ice, because it's attached to the shore. By spring, it can freeze six feet deep."

She stared down at the greaselike film on the water. It was the first floating veil of the whales' doom. Six feet of ice, she thought morosely. Ice as deep as a grave. "Hey." Billy cuffed her elbow playfully. "Don't look so sad. Anything can happen. Tomorrow, who knows?"

She shrugged, unable to speak. Both whales had disappeared below the swaying surface of the water. They would rise to breathe again in a few minutes. Today their predicament impressed her even more powerfully than before.

"Hey," Billy cajoled again, giving her elbow another poke. "Get your camera out. Take my picture. Make me famous. I hear you already made him famous." He nodded at Hal, who was testing the camera's focus.

If Hal had heard the boy's remark, he didn't allow it to register on his face. "Billy, get that hydrophone going. We need to monitor these guys."

"That's all you're going to do?" She faced Hal, her hands in her pockets. "Just videotape them and monitor them?" She knew she had no right to blame Hal, but her emotions were so tumultuous that she couldn't stop herself.

The smaller whale rose, making swells and shooting a triangle of spray into the air. Hal didn't bother to look at Jen. The slant of his mouth was both angry and sarcastic. "What am I supposed to do, Miss Martinson?"

She glared at him while he focused the camera on Doofus's snout. "Well, you could do something. They're going to die, and all you're going to do is record it for *science*." She said the word with maximum sarcasm.

"Look, I'd given anything I own to help them. You refuse to understand that. You just flat, pig-headed refuse. Move, will you? Goofus is going to surface right behind you."

She stepped out of the way. Behind her she heard the ripples and huge gasping noise that announced that the larger whale had risen. She pointed out to the lead, a dark crack in the distant ice. It gave off a frosty smoke. "Why don't you make that crack bigger? So they can get out?"

"I'm not God," he said.

"You don't have to be. Drop dynamite in the lead or something."

"Whales have sensitive hearing. We'd deafen them."

"Well, if you can't get the lead to come to them, why can't you take them to the lead?" countered Jen. "Make a path. More breathing holes. Something."

She looked at him pleadingly. She was angry with him, yet somehow, in spite of everything, she also believed in him. He was strong, he was intelligent, he understood the situation: surely he could change it. He might be maddening, but he could never be helpless. He could save the two trapped animals, she was certain, if he really put his mind to it.

"We've tried. You don't understand. These aren't bowheads. They're grays. Nothing we do for them works."

"Why not?"

He shook his head. "They're not built to survive an Arctic winter. We tried new breathing holes. They won't go to them. They don't understand what they're for. We could try to open a path with chain saws, but we don't know how the whales'd react. Besides, it'd take more man power, time and money than we've got. With the water freezing this fast it might not even be possible to keep a channel open."

"Too much money? You're making this a matter of money?"

"Look, the whole North Slope is a borough. It funds the research base, among other things. But it can't spend its whole budget on two whales. Not when the people up here need so much."

"But—how could anybody kill these animals? How could they allow it?"

He sighed in exasperation. "Jen, nobody wants the whales to die. Nobody. But the natives might vote to take them just to keep them from suffering. It's an emergency situation, and they'd clear it first with the Federal agency."

Jen narrowed her eyes. "Are you trying to foist the responsibility off on the Eskimos?"

The two whales took deep, ragged breaths, then sank beneath the dark water. Hal turned to her. "I'm not foisting anything off on anybody. These are facts, dammit."

"An icebreaker," Jen said with a sudden flash of inspiration. "Aren't there ships that plow through the ice? Can't you call an icebreaker?"

"No. This country only has two, both older than Methuselah, and the only one near us gets stuck in the ice every time it comes. It'd be stuck worse than the whales."

She was startled by the revelation. "It doesn't sound like much of an icebreaker."

"Tell Long John Blabbermouth about it. Maybe everybody'll call up the Coast Guard and gripe at them instead of me. I'm not personally responsible if these whales die. Can't you get that through your head?"

"You could be responsible for saving them. Can't you tranquilize them and move them? Get them out to sea?"

Hal gritted his teeth and looked heavenward. In the last fifteen minutes the sky had turned gray with thin clouds scudding across the sun. He could almost feel the temperature dropping. Things didn't look good; they were looking worse all the time.

He looked back at Jen, and the familiar vein jumped in his temple. "Nobody knows how to drug them, what dose to use. And if I did, how would we move them? Weave whale harnesses for them and *tow* them over the ice? Tie seabirds to them and fly them out?"

He turned from her to end the conversation. She was making him angry—at himself. He squinted up at the sky again. *Warm up, dammit,* he thought. *I've got whales here to keep alive.*

"I want you to know you're putting out some extremely negative vibrations," she said, "and I don't imagine they're doing these poor whales any good."

He swore under his breath. He wished he could magically transmit her back to California so she'd be thousands of miles away. He wished he'd never seen her. Most of all, he wished he didn't remember what her lips tasted like or the way her flesh felt beneath his fingertips.

He turned back to her. "Look—I'm not the only hope on earth for these whales." *It's got to be the weather,* he thought. *And the weather doesn't look good.*

"That's exactly what you are," she said, "their only hope on earth. Think of a way to save them. You have to." She looked so concerned that he forgot he was angry with her. She had so much emotion in her expression that it made his heart hurt as if a claw gripped it.

He turned away again. She wanted him to be a hero, and he couldn't. The cold was closing in like a pack of wolves. There would be no fighting it. If he could get the animals to move to another hole, then he might have a chance, a ghost of a chance. But they wouldn't move. Their fear paralyzed them.

He looked toward the horizon. The lead to the open sea was more than two miles away. It might as well have been two million.

SHORTLY AFTER NOON a figure appeared, riding from the west on a snow machine. It was Warren Tipana, Billy said, the hunter who had originally discovered the whales. Hal raised his arm in greeting, but when Warren dismounted the snow machine, he was not smiling. His face was grimly set.

Warren did not like to speak English, so Billy translated his uncle's messages. Warren had gone to the facility with a packet of notes for Hal from the mayor's office. Hal frowned and took the large yellow envelope.

"He says city hall's been getting calls all morning," Billy said, pushing back his unruly black forelock. "The phones ring all the time. People are saying not to let the whales die. The mayor is getting a very bad headache. Also, one of the whaling captains wants to know if he should call a meeting about whether to harvest the whales. He says a storm is coming. Also, four different television stations have asked the mayor for videotapes—would Dr. Bailey please supply?"

Billy went on.... Could Dr. Bailey also please release tapes for the radio stations and photographs for the newspapers? His Honor the mayor beseeched Dr. Bailey to make it clear that the people of Ultima were as concerned as everyone else about the welfare of the whales.

Warren, bearing all the urgent messages from Ultima, had set out from the mayor's office and gone to A.R.F. in search of Hal. There he found Hal's office in more of an uproar than the mayor's.

Seven television stations and two networks had called the facility, asking for videotapes. A prominent Alaskan senator had called from Washington, asking what, in this crisis, he could do for his state, his voters and his whales. In addition, LiveWorld, a militant group of environmentalists, had threatened to start legal action to keep the whales from being killed.

"Damn!" Exasperation crossed Hal's face. "I've got a couple of poor worn-out whales stuck in the ice and people want to make it political?"

Jen was horrified, too. Warren had brought a second fat packet of messages and requests and threats from the base. She had never expected such an outpouring of interest about the whales, and worse, none of the interest was helpful. It seemed only to be adding to the complexity and unpleasantness of the situation.

Hal glanced upward, his brow furrowed. The sky had turned an even more ominous gray, and a wind was rising from the north. He pulled up the hood of his parka. "It's getting colder," he said to nobody in particular.

Jen looked at the whales. Goofus, the larger, bobbed near the edge of the breathing hole, his speckled snout high in the air. As usual, his almost human eye seemed to be watching the people on the ice, as if he, too, waited for them to do something.

The smaller whale, Doofus, seemed listless and kept farther from the humans. The younger animal was clearly the weaker one. Its fear and fatigue wrenched Jen and she wondered how long its strength could last.

Beside her Hal fanned through the messages that Warren had brought. "This is crazy," he muttered. "Crazy!"

Warren, watching the dark clouds that drifted on the horizon, said something in Eskimo. "There'll be snow within a few days," Billy said, exploring the bleak sky.

Jen blinked hard. She told herself that it was the cold and not tears that stung her eyes. The little whale, Doofus, looked too tired to last much longer.

Beside her, Hal stood, shaking his head as he looked through the sheaf of notes. "Crazy," he repeated. "The world's gone crazy."

BACK AT THE FACILITY her phone rang as she let herself into her room. She threw off her parka, flinging it to the bed. She picked up the telephone and said hello more curtly than she'd meant.

"By the almighty dollar, what have you done?" demanded her grandfather. "Your whales are the talk of California. Gad! You're an impossible girl."

Exasperated and bone tired, Jen sat down on the edge of the bed. "You're impossible yourself. How do you dare call Hal Bailey and try to *bribe* him to send me home?" No wonder Hal had no respect for her, she thought miserably.

"That blasted Bailey! The man was impertinent to me. Doesn't the fool realize I could buy and sell him?"

"No," Jen replied, "apparently he doesn't." *And you're wrong, Dagobert. This is one man you couldn't buy. Or sell.*

"I just wanted you home, sweety," Dagobert said with gruff affection. "And the Bailey man doesn't want you there. He made that clear. Come on home. You're not working for Ferd any more. There's no need for you to be there."

Jen put one hand to her forehead. Her skull ached, her skin felt hot, her mouth dry. Nobody thought she should be in Alaska except herself and Walter Stonebridger. "I'm staying here. I work for the Redwood City *Sentinel* now."

"The *Sentinel*? You most certainly will not!" Dagobert objected. "Just two months ago they called me 'a grasping old robber-baron.'"

Jen's temples throbbed. "You *liked* being called a robber-baron. You said it put you in the company of the greats. Face it, Dagobert, a lot of people don't like your ecological policies—or lack of them."

"Pah! When I was a young man, nobody bothered about such things. Now I bend over backward to please everybody."

She thought of Hal's opinion of her family, and her head hurt worse. "You don't bend far enough. Your reputation is still terrible."

Dagobert scoffed. "I could be more popular than breathing, with those sassy ecologists, if I wanted. I could be their darling in a week. I could do more good in one day—if I chose—than the *Sentinel* can in a year with its sentimental slop. Stop working for them. This instant."

"No. They hired me."

"If you have to do this fool story before you come home, do it for Ferd. He'll hire you back."

"No. Never again."

"Use this story for public relations for the family name then. You're the one who thinks my reputation needs to be prettied up. Do you like the sound of public relations work? I could create a special job for you. With a special office—a penthouse. And I've been chatting with that president's son. He'd like to meet you."

She pressed her hand harder against her forehead. "I'm not working for you, either," she said as firmly as she could. "I don't want to meet the president's son. I want to live my own life."

"I can *make* you be my public relations person, whether you like it or not," Dagobert warned. "And in the meantime, Ferd can send a real reporter up there to scoop you. Even a fifth rate paper like the *Sentinel* won't need you then. Stop defying me. It was cute at first but I'm tired of it."

He hung up. Jen put the receiver back in its cradle and stared at it. She wanted to lie down on the bed, curl up and cry into the pillow with frustration. But that, somehow, would be a victory for Dagobert. At least he had told her one sensible thing—to stay away from Hal.

Hal, she thought. He wasn't going to like what she was about to do. She would do it anyway. She had to.

She shook her head to clear it and dialed the Redwood City *Sentinel*. She reached Walter F. Stonebridger and gave him the facts, as she knew them—even the unpleasant ones.

"People are eating this up, Martinson," Stonebridger rasped in his smoke-and-whiskey voice. "You've been blessed. You're in the right place at the right time. The AP wires are going to pick up this story. You can bet on it. Your career is made. When you come back to California, you want to work full-time for me?"

No, Jen said politely, she didn't think so. It wouldn't be right, considering the *Sentinel's* stand against her grandfather, and besides she wasn't coming back to California.

"Just using us now to make a point to the old scoundrel?" Stonebridger asked.

"Maybe," Jen said. She didn't even know any longer. A familiar lump arose in her throat. The wind had risen, rattling at her window. She thought, for the thousandth time, of the trapped whales and the ice creeping in to claim them.

"Hey," Stonebridger assured her, "don't worry about it. Everybody uses everybody. That's how it works."

She told him goodbye and that she'd keep him informed. She hung up.

She rose and moved to the window. Beyond the compound of the facility, the featureless landscape stretched out. The sun, a ghostly disk, was already sinking beneath the southern horizon. North, where the sky was darkest, the two whales were fighting the currents to stay in their breathing hole so that they might cling to survival a little longer. Jen shook her head helplessly. Could it really help if the world knew their story? Or had she simply bungled everything and no good would come of it?

When Hal didn't come to take her to the dining room, she went alone, but quickly wished she hadn't. Everyone there, including two women she hadn't seen before, stared at her with a mixture of curiosity and thinly veiled dislike. Nobody spoke to her. Nobody so much as said hello.

She found herself smiling automatically at Arnold, who simply looked at her stonily, filled her plate, then stared at her again with the same unfriendly black eyes. The smile died on her face.

Hal was nowhere to be seen, nor was Billy. She sat alone and no one approached her. But icy stares were leveled at her and their message was clear—she had unsettled life at the facility, she had brought chaos raining down on it, and now she was its outcast. Emotional cold as intense as the physical cold outside frosted the air of the room. Unable to stand it, Jen stood up and headed for the door, her supper barely touched.

At ten o'clock a knock rattled her door. She answered it with trepidation, wondering if the facility had sent an emissary to ask her to leave.

Hal stood there with a sandwich, chips and can of cola. "I heard you didn't eat tonight," he said. "I was in Ultima. Talking to the mayor."

He stared at her, and complicated emotions seemed to cross his face. When he spoke again, his voice was harsh. "Look, I guess you found out you're not popular around here. You've set this place on its ear. You've pretty well disrupted everything."

She kept her expression under rigid control. "People make it clear. Yes. I'm . . . sorry."

He shook his head. "I have too much to do to baby-sit you. I don't intend to do it again. Here's something to eat. After this you're on your own."

Jen thanked him, but sat down on the edge of the bed, too dispirited to eat. "I just keep thinking about the whales."

She expected him to go, but he did not. He sat in the room's single chair, unasked. "Worry won't help. Eat, will you? I told you, I can't keep on taking care of you."

"Nobody asked you to."

"Wrong. Keenan did."

"I didn't come to cause you trouble. Or anybody else. I wouldn't stay except I have a job to do. What did the mayor say?"

He gave her a half smile, but it was bitter. "Why do you want to know? To spread it all over California? Thanks to you, this town has a major image problem. A bunch of people are expecting us to save those whales. I don't know that it can be done."

"What's the weather like?" she asked, listening once more to the wind shake the window pane.

"Cold. Twenty below."

Jen felt him watching her, but she didn't want to look at him. Sometimes she thought she saw a trace of tenderness in his eyes, and it always hurt when she realized she was mistaken. "Will they survive the night? The whales?"

"Probably." His voice was clipped, without emotion.

"Just 'probably'?" Jen darted him an accusing glance. "You're hard-hearted. You know that, of course."

"I'm realistic, that's all. Eat, will you?"

She shook her head. "I'm not hungry. I keep thinking about them. About how sad their breathing sounds."

He shrugged. "Go hungry. See what good it does."

She shifted uneasily on the bed. The little room felt as if it had shrunk and had become too warm and too small. Hal seemed to be there only to make her miserable. "Why don't you go?" she asked. "Haven't you seen enough of me for one day?"

He looked away, disgust etched on his face. "Yes. I have." He stood. "I came because I was concerned about you. But I don't think it's appropriate to keep up this—this association between us. We don't exactly bring out the best in each other."

She blinked in surprise that he felt the slightest bit of consideration for her.

"I'm putting Billy in charge of you. In deference to Keenan, you'll remain a guest of this facility. But from now on you get the same information from me that any other outsider gets. Before, I just had one reporter to deal with. Now I've got a passel. What'd be best is if you'd just go home. Especially in light of how people around here feel about you."

She still refused to look at him. "Oh, stop lecturing. Just leave, will you? I'd rather talk to Billy anyway. At least he's human."

She tossed her head and kept staring pointedly away from him, waiting for him to go. He made a strange ache fill her chest; an empty sensation spread dismally through her.

She got up, taking care to keep her distance from him. She went to the window and pushed aside the drapes. The northern lights wavered in the blackness, as strange and beautiful as the first night she had seen them. The ache in her chest grew, choked her with sadness. "Please," she said. "Just go away. Please."

She remembered her grandfather's words: "Stay away from him." Now she wouldn't have to. Hal would stay away from her. She kept staring out at the lights, and she swallowed hard.

She respected Hal, she believed in his strength and above all in his integrity, his devotion to his job, but she wished he could be simply human. A creature with emotions. Kindness. Feelings.

She felt infinitely relieved when he left the room. But she felt overwhelmed by loneliness, too.

HAL STALKED down the hall. He didn't even know why he'd come, or why he'd tried to talk to her. He'd wanted to tell her that maybe there was a chance for the whales, a slim one. But he hadn't. He had no right to give her any false hope.

He'd wanted to tell her he was sorry for what had happened in the dining room—that everybody was tired, upset and apprehensive, that was all. But he'd said none of it.

He ground his teeth, realizing again that he should never have had anything to do with her from the start. The Martinson family stood for everything he disliked. Too much money, too much power, too little concern for the earth's fragile environment.

She had blundered into a bad situation and without half trying had made it worse. She had entered the scene on a whim and remained out of sheer stubbornness. Keenan didn't want her, but he didn't want to hurt her, either. It was all insane.

Worst, she consistently turned Hal, a normally rational and patient man, into an unreasoning grump. She ended up making him angry at everything, including himself.

No, he amended. That wasn't the worst. The worst was that he found that he desired her as much as he disliked what she stood for.

Against all logic she made him want to do heroic things: move mountains, open paths through the frozen sea, perform impossible feats. He found himself angry that he was only a man. And only human.

CHAPTER EIGHT

IT WAS AS IF JEN HAD, without meaning to, opened a Pandora's box of troubles that swarmed, stinging, biting and darkening the air.

Confusion swelled the next day as the world turned its attention to the whales. Press services picked up Jen's report for the *Sentinel*. Papers everywhere reprinted it. Television networks carried the facility's footage of the whales, and their plight was shown from coast to coast and beyond.

The phones jangled incessantly. The callers questioned, advised, wished the scientists well, lectured, wept, harangued, threatened, pried, prayed and swore. So many reporters demanded to talk to Hal that his secretary lost count.

Almost everyone at the facility was harried and a bit wild-eyed. Too many in the outside world were convinced that the scientists of A.R.F. and the Eskimos were about to murder the whales in cold blood.

Hal stayed calm but forbiddingly grim. He took the most crucial calls and tried to deal with the ones that were threatening or emotional so that his staff wouldn't have to. The whale story was swiftly turning into a full-fledged media circus. Hal, against his will, was cast as ringmaster, the man who must keep control.

That evening Jen passed him in the hall as she came from the facility's library. Although he had avoided her all day, she could not keep herself from stopping him. His expression was aloof, contained.

She knew it was useless to apologize, but she had to try. "I never knew this would happen—all this . . ." She gestured helplessly, trying to indicate the chaos that had descended on the base.

Hal's face remained rigid. "The press is a loaded gun. You played with it, and it went off."

She winced. "And it was aimed at Ultima. I'm sorry—"

"Apologize to the staff, not me. They're bearing the brunt. Regular work's totally disrupted. They're off schedule, off balance and overworked. And the mayor's office is going crazy, too."

"I didn't mean . . ."

His mouth curled. "What you *meant* doesn't matter. We have to contend with what you *did*."

"Look—I'm trying to tell things exactly as they are. It's just that people respond with their hearts instead of their heads—they get so emotionally involved they overreact—"

"You're using this story to make your mark, and you've put this town in the impossible position where it has to save the whales—a job that nobody knows how to do. Now we either think of a way to use the trouble, or the trouble uses us. I don't like being used."

Jen stared at him, wounded and angered. "I never meant to use anybody. And what do you mean, *use* the trouble?"

His gaze was as unnervingly steady as ever. "Somewhere in this mess, this ungodly mess, there may be some way to help those whales. It'll probably be a small opportunity and it'll probably pass quickly. It's my job to find it and use it. If that means using you, I'll do that, too. So save your apologies. We're past that stage. Way past it."

Jen tensed, recalling what Walter Stonebridger had said, that everybody uses everybody. "You mean you might be able to use this publicity? How?"

"I don't know how. I don't know if I can. All I know is, when there's trouble, you can either let it beat you down or you can grab on and twist it to your advantage."

"But—" Jen began.

He cut her off. "You want me to save those whales? Tell your damn paper we need help. The whales won't move by themselves, and we've got no means to move them. If nobody's going to do anything about it, then tell them to get off my back and let me work at it. I've got better things to do than answer phones."

Hal's secretary appeared at the other end of the hall, looking distraught. "Dr. Bailey—there you are—thank goodness. There's a phone call for you from Washington, D.C. And you're supposed to call California immediately. Also, a newspaper from London called. And one from Australia."

He left Jen standing there, looking after him. Stung, she turned and hurried toward her room. Tears welled in her eyes. The story was turning into a big one, a ridiculously big one that accomplished nothing.

Back in her room she called Walter F. Stonebridger for the second time that evening. "Is there a new development?" he asked.

"No. Listen," she said desperately, "Dr. Bailey needs help. The people of Ultima need help if these animals are going to be saved."

"What else is new, Martinson? Every time he talks to a reporter he says that. What's he expect, a miracle?"

"Maybe," Jen countered. "Why not?"

"Because," Stonebridger said, "there are only two possible miracles. One is to get an ice cutter there. Impossible. The closest one is Soviet, and it has to have two weeks' government clearance to come into U.S. waters—no exceptions. The other is that the weather improves, but you've got storm warnings like you've never seen. Too bad, but your job is to give me all the drama to the end. People are eating this up."

Jen hung up, frustration mounting. Nobody anywhere seemed able to help. But the blame would not fall on nature, which had trapped the whales, but on Ultima, which was helpless to save them. Stonebridger, sitting safely in California, saw it only as a "drama," a way to sell newspapers. Jen was suddenly tired of the newspaper business, bone tired. She didn't want to report facts. She wanted to change them.

Her phone jangled. She snatched it up. "Hello?"

"Hello," purred Dagobert. "Tired of the newspaper business yet?"

"No," she lied.

"Tired of the cold? Ready to come home to your granddaddy?"

This time she answered with complete conviction. "No. For the hundredth time."

"You might as well give up, Jen." His tone softened a degree. "You're about to be outclassed. Ferd's sending a real reporter up there."

"Fine. He'll get the same story I get. No progress. The weather's getting worse. The whales need help."

"Help?" Dagobert's tone became so bright he almost chirped. "Did you say 'help'? Are you asking for help, sweetheart?"

"No, I'm not."

"Too bad. I could dispatch my biologists from Prudhoe Bay—send them to help that mouthy Bailey. They're experts."

"Dr. Bailey's expert enough," she retorted. "He's smart, and he understands the situation, and he doesn't need strangers barging in trying to tell him what to do—"

"What's this? You're not getting involved with him, are you? I forbid it. I called him again today, to *order* him to send you home. He told me not to tie up his line with trivia—and hung up on me. Doesn't he know I can make him grovel if I want?"

"Dagobert, nobody who ever lived is going to make Hal Bailey *grovel*. He doesn't care about our family problems, and at this point, neither do I. I just want the whales free."

"You care about those two blubber-heads more than about *me*," accused Dagobert. "You're a selfish, headstrong and unnatural child."

"I won't feel guilty about this, and you can't make—"

"Don't *ever* tell me what I can or can't do," Dagobert snapped. "I can make you do whatever I choose. I can have you kissing the hem of my garment—and have your precious Bailey doing the same. You'll see. I can make you dance to the tune I call, young lady. And it'll be for your own good." He hung up loudly, to show her he meant business.

Jen set her teeth, her ear ringing. She put her head into her hands. She knew Dagobert well, and she knew he had reached the end of his patience. He would come after her full force now. She felt as trapped as the whales.

THE NEXT MORNING, Billy took Jen out on the ice again. He was the only person at the base who was friendly to her. Other staff members ignored her or cast looks of anger or resentment her way.

Of all the people at the facility, Billy alone managed to see humor in the situation and to joke about it. But when he took Jen out on the ice, even he turned grim.

The cold had increased, the ice built up more thickly. Hour by hour the breathing hole shrank. The whales, fighting the current to keep in the safety of their breathing area, were visibly weaker.

Billy shook his head. "We're going to lose them."

The morning was dark and the air brittle with cold. Jen felt sick. Little Doofus's nose had turned paler and splotchier. He was developing frostbite around one of his cuts, and his breathing sounded labored. "This is terrible," she said.

Billy's eyes met hers. "My mother says it's silly to make such an uproar over animals. But you can't look at them and not be sorry for them."

"I know." Jen dropped to her knees and reached out a mittened hand to stroke Goofus's barnacled face. He permitted it, which always awed her.

She looked across the breathing hole to where Hal stood in a small knot of people. She knew she had made his life hellishly complicated, and the fact increased her sense of unhappiness and isolation.

Publicity was already drawing strangers to Ultima, and Jen was now no longer the only interloper on the scene.

Reporters had arrived that morning from Anchorage with arrangements to supply both the *Anchorage Daily News* and *The New York Times* with stories. It was rumored that reporters from Seattle, San Francisco and Juneau were due within hours.

Morning had also seen the arrival of a round little man named Bartwick from an important federal bureau. He brought two veterinarians with him, and he now walked back and forth on the ice, squinting at the whales with an official squint.

Billy looked rueful. "Poor Hal. This ice is gonna get crowded before it's over. A bunch—a whole bunch—more people are due tomorrow. Warren Tipana still says the kindest thing would be to kill the whales. Other people say we don't dare. Everybody in the country would hate us."

Jen looked at him in alarm. "More people still? How many more? How do you know?"

"I called the base on the truck's CB. Just now."

Jen's gaze traveled back to Hal, the man who always had to stand, unmoved, at the center of this storm of confusion. The wind stirred the brown fur around his hood as he tried to explain something to one of the veterinarians, who kept interrupting. Hal kept his patience with remarkable restraint, she thought, but he didn't need still more people to contend with.

Billy recited a depressingly long list of reporters, officials, dignitaries and activists about to descend on Ultima. Television crews would arrive, even a film crew. Finally there were representatives coming from MaLaBar Oil in Prudhoe Bay. If a spotlight was shining, Billy said cynically, MaLaBar Oil wanted to seize its share of publicity.

Once more Jen felt sick. Dagobert's corporation owned a large chunk of MaLaBar, and he hadn't waited for her to ask for help. He saw an opportunity and was taking it, determined to exploit the situation for all the publicity it was worth. She could already see the headlines: Concerned Oilmen Rush To Stranded Whales. Hal, who felt no love for the oil companies, would despise her for bringing this latest development down on him. "MaLaBar? Oh, no."

Billy nodded. "Weird, huh?"

She stole another glance across the dark water at Hal. Briefly his eyes met hers. She experienced the familiar shock at their blueness, their coolness, their steadiness. Then he turned away, as if he had seen nobody where she stood.

"Yes," Jen said to Billy, pretending the moment hadn't shaken her. "Any time the oil companies and environmentalists are on the same side, it's strange."

"And Eskimos," added Billy. "We've had our differences with both of them. At least everybody's coming together for once in a single cause. You've got yourself a story now."

Yes. I've got myself a story now, thought Jen. It was making Ultima insane and Hal Bailey's life sheer hell, and it was a story that might end as unhappily as possible. She should never have started it.

She held herself more stiffly against the cold. She could not dwell on the negative, and she would not quit. Hal could hate her and resent her with all his stony heart. Dagobert could marshall his considerable forces and sent them marching against her. The whole world could stand on its head. She had started this. She would see it out to the end.

THE NEXT DAY madness reigned. Jen was no longer alone in her section of the compound, for Bartwick, the Federal man, and his two veterinarians had moved into the other guest rooms. Jen had found herself sharing a bathroom with the younger vet, who turned out to be more lustful than neighborly.

Unhappy at finding himself in the far reaches of the Arctic, he had consoled himself with vodka. No liquor was sold in Ultima itself, but he had brought his own plentiful supply. In his cups, he decided she was irresistible. Jen locked her door to the bathroom, but he stood next to it, loudly serenading her with risqué songs and telling her what he would like to do to her.

She had no choice but to complain next morning to Billy, who had no choice but to report it to Hal. Hal gritted his teeth and told Billy to move Jen into Keenan's apartment where she would be safe.

Keenan's apartment was next to Hal's, and Hal looked disgusted at the prospect of having her near. As the morning wore on, he looked disgusted about everything.

People were arriving in hordes. At breakfast Jen sat alone in the dining hall, staring into the murky depths of her coffee. Hal, too, sat alone at another table, frowning over sheets of weather information. The weather, she thought hopelessly, must be getting worse, which meant that the whales were in more trouble than ever.

Hal's secretary hurried in, whispered intently with him and bustled out again. Hal glanced across the room at Jen, his face hard. *Oh, no,* she thought, *another emergency.*

He pushed his weather reports into a folder and headed out the door, his long strides indicating that there was indeed a new crisis.

A moment later Billy entered and came to Jen's table. "A reporter from San Francisco just got here, and he's looking for you. His name's Finnegan. Do you want him to find you?"

Jen shook her head no. Finnegan was a hard, cynical little man with a withered face and a withered soul. She knew he had been sent by Ferd and probably Dagobert to intimidate her, to shake what little confidence she had left. She didn't want to face him yet. "Sit down," she told Billy. "Please. I need to see a friendly face."

"Me, too." Billy gave her a wry smile. "All of a sudden there're too many strange ones around."

Later, as Billy drove her out to the whales, he told her that five environmentalists were arriving today. "One's great, Hal says, three others are okay, but one's a real nut case. He hates all Eskimos and anyone else who hunts or even eats meat. I don't know what he thinks we're supposed to do in this climate—grow mangoes? Eat snow?"

The ice was no longer clean and isolated. Vehicles crowded it and had scarred it with tracks. Reporters, photographers and videographers came and went, mingling with curiosity seekers from Ultima and surrounding villages.

Hal didn't arrive until half past noon. He came alone, and he did not speak to Jen. He ordered people to get back from the breathing hole, said there were too many crowding around, frightening the whales.

Shortly after one in the afternoon, Jen's fears were realized when two men from MaLaBar Oil's base in Prudhoe Bay arrived on the ice. They descended grandly from a taxicab they had taken from the Ultima airport. Jen cringed.

MaLaBar's representatives were a large jolly biologist with a black mustache and a short wiry spokesman with a blond beard. Jen watched as the spokesman gathered a group of reporters around him. She knew he would lecture them on MaLaBar's deep and abiding interest in protecting nature.

She crowded in with the others, although she had no faith that he would say one thing worth listening to. She was sure he was there for political reasons only.

"I am LaMont Marcuse," the spokesman began. "The MaLaBar Oil Corporation is concerned about our unfortunate friends here and has sent its top biologist, Dr. Stanley Frank, to examine the situation and offer his expert advice."

Marcuse tried hard to look dignified, but his nose was red with cold, and he couldn't keep his teeth from chattering. "It's Dr. Frank's learned opinion that the research facility and the people of Ultima should do *everything* in their power to keep these whales alive—in hopes that the weather changes, breaking the ice and freeing the whales. I repeat, A.R.F. and Ultima must do everything to keep the whales alive while MaLaBar studies the situation."

Drat, Jen thought, gritting her teeth. He wasn't saying anything new. All he was doing was thrusting more responsibility on Hal and Ultima while MaLaBar took whatever glory it could.

Her awareness prickled when Hal appeared behind Marcuse, clamping his gloved hand on the little man's shoulder. "Excuse me." He looked at Marcuse, but spoke loudly so all the reporters could hear. "You're offering nothing but talk, Marcuse. Talk's cheap. MaLaBar might be able to volunteer something more valuable."

Jen's ears pricked up. Hal's voice had an official ring, as if he were making an announcement. "I'd like to ask you about something while the press is here." He paused, and this time glanced directly at Jen. "Make sure this hits the California papers, will you, Martinson? The Californians keep saying how concerned they are. We'll see."

Jen's cheeks burned. What was he up to now, she wondered, and why had he singled her out? Did he dislike her so intensely that he didn't mind revealing it in public?

"This morning at eight o'clock," Hal said, "I had a call. I was informed MaLaBar Oil has an ice-cutting hoverbarge in storage. It can cut through two feet of ice, maybe more. If MaLaBar's really so concerned about these whales, why don't they send the barge to free them?"

A barge, Jen thought. *A barge that could plow through the ice. It could open a path to the sea.* The thought was like the sun breaking through the cloud-bound sky.

The other reporters reacted immediately. "Barge? You mean an ice cutter?" "At Prudhoe?" "Have you asked them about it?"

Hal held up his hand for silence. "I've called three times. I can't get anything out of them. It's not an ice cutter, it's not half as powerful, not a quarter. But if they've got it, it's the closest thing we'll get."

Marcuse's mouth dropped open, and his eyes glazed slightly. "I—a hoverbarge? I don't know—I wasn't notified—I'll have to contact—"

The other reporters crowded more tightly around Marcuse and Hal, jostling them. Questions peppered the air. "Why've they kept this quiet?" "You've asked them three times?" "They're not talking?"

Hal stepped back and stood taller to deal with the crowd. "I'm told that seven years ago MaLaBar had it built, but never used it. It's been in mothballs. Yes—I've phoned MaLaBar three times asking for information. They won't give any. If this barge exists, and if it works, it could be our one chance to save these animals."

Jen stood back as the other reporters crowded closer to Hal. *Power play,* she thought, and smiled with satisfaction.

Hal had watched and waited, and at last he had found it: a way to help the whales. MaLaBar Oil, in turn, had tried to be coy, and he had retaliated by bringing the press to bear on them. She smiled again. For a man who didn't like the media, Hal knew exactly how to use it. MaLaBar didn't dare turn him down now that the public knew of the barge's existence.

"A hoverbarge that cuts ice," Billy muttered. "I kind of remembering hearing about that, years ago. Nobody ever knew if it worked."

"It has to work," Jen said. "It has to."

Hal held up his hand again for quiet.

"One thing I know about this barge is that it can't move under its own power. It has to be towed. By helicopter. MaLaBar may not have a 'copter big enough. But the National Guard does. I'd like to ask, publicly, that it be sent if MaLaBar will dispatch the barge. If enough people pull together, maybe we can get these whales to freedom. It's going to take a cooperative effort, a big one. Nobody's going to do it alone."

A television reporter elbowed to the front of the crowd, his cameraman behind him. "Bailey, you're asking for help from MaLaBar *and* the National Guard? For a couple of animals? Isn't it going to cost a lot of money?"

Hal gave a philosophical shrug. "Who can put a price on something like this?"

Another reporter began to interrogate Marcuse. "Is it true? Does MaLaBar have the barge? Does it work? Will they send it?"

Marcuse still looked stunned by Hal's revelation. "I—I wasn't aware of the existence of such a craft. I need to check. But MaLaBar Oil is committed to ecology. It will do anything—within reason—to free these whales. MaLaBar Oil will do—well, whatever it can." He swallowed hard, clearly worried about exceeding the limits of his power.

Jen's hopes soared drunkenly. Maybe MaLaBar could accomplish the impossible. It had the money and equipment to do so. It had the motive as well: public relations. But her hopes fell when she saw Hal's face. He looked neither convinced nor optimistic, only fiercely determined.

As the reporters converged on Marcuse, Hal muttered, "That's all I've got to say." He broke free from the group and headed toward his truck. Jen hesitated a moment, then dashed after him. When she caught up with him, he barely glanced at her.

"Shouldn't you be asking Marcuse for details?" he jibed. "Trying to pin him down?"

"You pinned him nicely, thanks. If MaLaBar has the barge, they'll have to send it. The public would raise a terrible outcry if they refused."

Hal reached the truck. He stopped and looked back toward the crowds of people milling on the ice. "A circus," he muttered. "It's turned into the devil's own circus."

"But isn't it all right if it helps you save the whales?" She studied the solemn, almost angry set of his face.

"This is a long shot, that's all. The barge's been in storage seven years. Who knows what shape it's in? Plus, the Guard has to agree to tow it two hundred miles through a sea of ice. Even if we get it here and it works, it'll leave so much broken ice, the whales may not be able to follow it out. They could get cut up worse than they are now. Besides, there's a ridge forming out there that could be too thick for it to cut through."

"But—" Jen protested, confused "—if you don't think it'll work, why'd you set the wheels in motion?"

He glanced at her, then back at the teeming ice. "A bad chance is better than no chance."

Her giddy hopes wavered. "But you know it exists. You know that MaLaBar has it."

"I got a tip by phone. It involved you, in fact." His eyes settled on her with disturbing steadiness.

"Me?" Jen blinked in amazement.

"You. Why the surprise? Everyplace you go, trouble follows."

"What have I got to do with it?"

The wind rose, howling across the frozen plains. "I don't think I want to know. Your grandfather called me this morning. Again."

Jen tensed. She should have known. Dagobert was ready to corner her, he was moving in. A fearful hollowness filled her. "My grandfather?"

"He told me about the hovercraft. He said he could get MaLaBar to send it—if two criteria were met. First, quote, 'if Jennifer asks me to do it... asks me nicely' unquote. Second, if I make a public statement about how well your grandfather—and MaLaBar—serve environmental interests. He said he'd send me the text of what he wanted me to say."

She paled, more shaken still. Dagobert was using his influence with MaLaBar as blackmail. He would stop at nothing to get her home. "But—I can't ask him for anything—it's impossible."

She looked back toward the breathing hole, her gaze frantic. She knew if asking Dagobert for help was the only way to free the whales, she would have to ask. There was no choice.

"Too proud?" Hal's voice was sarcastic. "That's fine. I've got pride, too. I won't bow down to Dagobert Martinson or MaLaBar or anybody else. And I won't lie for them. He wants to play games? All right—but he'll play fair. Or I'll expose him for the power-hungry old fox he is. I've got enough reporters around to do it. If he doesn't come through by tonight, *I'll* call Long John Silverburg. We'll see how your grandfather likes *that*."

Jen stared at him, dumbfounded. Her grandfather had set a trap for her. He had set it cleverly and neatly, and he meant for it to snap on her. He wanted her to humble herself to ask him to send the hoverbarge. Hal, too, was supposed to find himself in Dagobert's power and be brought to his knees.

But Hal had struck back so quickly and so hard that Dagobert's head would swim. Hal had put MaLaBar—and Dagobert—in such a position that they couldn't dare refuse to cooperate. Hal had defied Dagobert, and it would infuriate the older man, truly infuriate him, Jen knew.

"My grandfather won't like this. You're making a powerful enemy."

"A powerful enemy is the only kind worth having, Miss Martinson. A weak one isn't any challenge."

He opened the door of the truck and got in. He glanced one more time at the carnivallike scene on the ice, then angrily put the truck into gear and drove off.

She stared after him, her heart beating hard. Hal might just have saved her from Dagobert's clutches. He wouldn't know that, of course, and if he knew, he wouldn't care. Still, she couldn't help smiling. "Dagobert," she said, "I think you've finally met your match."

CHAPTER NINE

SHE HAD EXPECTED Dagobert to be as furious as some old troll in a fairy tale who has had his plans foiled and his treasure stolen. Instead when she talked to him that evening, he was eerily calm.

"The boy's smart. Tougher than I thought," he said of Hal. "Well. This could get interesting."

"He's not a boy. He's a man," Jen said. "Don't push him, Dagobert. He'll push back."

"Oh? Sounds as if you'd like that. Sounds as if you like *him*. Typical. I tell you not to do something, you do it. I'd better get you home among your own kind, where you can't get in trouble."

"Dagobert, you can't make me ask for that barge. If you hold back on it, everyone will think you're the meanest man in America and that MaLaBar's the worst corporate villain in history."

"I wouldn't dream of not sending it," he protested. "The other stockholders would raise Cain. Bailey's made it so that it has to be sent. So it costs a few hundred thousand. No problem. I just hope it works, that's all."

"What do you mean?" He was up to something, she knew it.

"Nothing. I just found out last night about the thing myself. You know oil companies—they like big toys. This barge is a big toy that everyone was eager to forget. Know why MaLaBar never used it? They didn't have anything big enough to tow it. Oh, corporations, corporations—imagine building a barge so big you can't tow it. Tsk."

"You mean you dangled this thing like bait in front of everybody, but it won't work?" she demanded.

"I don't know if it works. We'll see."

Jen shook her head in despair. "Don't you ever get tired of trying to manipulate people?"

"Yes. Come home and I'll stop."

"No. I've got a story to cover."

"Ah... but how will it end? Can that fool barge actually save those whales? Perhaps they can't be saved at all. How sad. Your friend Bailey won't seem so heroic then, will he? He'll just be a chump on an iceberg, and a failed chump at that. He'll get his barge, all right. But we'll have to wait to see what good it does. You may need much more help than it can give you. But—you'll have to ask me for it. And remember—nobody loves you like your granddaddy."

"More help—?" Jen didn't know what he meant, but her question was interrupted by an abrupt *click*. As usual, he had cut off any further argument by hanging up.

What did he mean—ask him for "much more help"? If the barge didn't save the whales, nothing could. He was bluffing, she told herself. He had reached the limits of his power, so he was playing mind games, trying to keep her off balance.

She stood, smoothing her hair and taking up her shoulder bag. Billy had promised to have supper with her so that she wouldn't have to brave the dining hall alone. She went to meet him, worrying all the way about what Dagobert had said. If the barge didn't work, they were back to where they started—helpless. The whales were trapped as badly as before, and their time was running out.

Billy waited for her, nursing a cup of coffee. She tried to ignore the hostile looks of the other diners as she crossed the room and sat down.

Billy's face was unnaturally glum. "Hi," was all he said. When she told him MaLaBar was sending the barge, he shrugged and tried to smile, but his smile was slightly sick. She studied him with mounting concern. "Oh, please, Billy, don't be depressed. Do you hate this, always being seen with me? I know it's my fault that things got out of hand. All I can say is I'm sorry."

He shrugged again. "What's done is done." He stared into his coffee.

"Billy," she said, desperation in her voice, "What's wrong? What is it?"

He looked away. "Nothing."

"Billy!"

"All right. Hal said he didn't think MaLaBar could get the barge here in time—even if it works perfectly. The temperature's dropping again and a storm's on the way. The hole's going to close. Soon. We're probably going to have to put Goofus and Doofus out of their misery. The Federal man will okay the whaling captains' doing it. They're the only ones with the equipment."

"Oh." It was all she could say.

Billy took a deep breath. "It's not just killing them that bothers me. It's that *we'll* have to do it. The Eskimos. We'll get blamed. Have you met the environmentalist that calls himself Leafy Ted? He thinks we're murderers because most of us have to hunt to live. We'll be the heavies, and the people from MaLaBar will come out smelling like roses. *They* cared about the whales. *They* tried to help. We're nothing but killers."

Billy shook his head again. She patted his hand, but lapsed into silence, unable to think of anything comforting to say. He was right. If the barge couldn't make it in time, the whales would die, but MaLaBar would still look good; it had at least tried. The Eskimos, on the other hand, would seem like pillagers of helpless wildlife.

She looked up and saw Hal heading toward their table. He wore faded denims that emphasized his leanness, and a blue checked shirt that made his eyes even more vivid than usual. He bore down on them purposefully, his gaze trained on Billy.

He put his hand on the boy's shoulder. "Go get into the warmest gear you can find. I need volunteers to work on the ice tonight. You just volunteered."

Billy looked up in disbelief. "Go back out there? Man, it's dark. I haven't even been home."

"Look," Hal said. "The right strings have been pulled. MaLaBar's sending the barge. The National Guard volunteered its biggest helicopter to tow it. There's a chance in a thousand they might pull this rescue off. But it'll take two days to get the barge in shape, and at least a full day to tow it. It's starting to storm, and we've got to keep that breathing hole open till the barge gets here."

"At night, man?" Billy protested. "It's going to be murder out there."

"A company in Wisconsin shipped us two ice fans. They use them in marinas, to keep boats from freezing in. I don't know if they'll work this far north, but we can try them. We can take a generator and plug them in. And chain saws. We're going to have to cut the ice back."

Billy groaned. He shook his head again but rose to obey. Hal gave him a hearty slap on the back. "Good kid. Meet me at the motor pool in fifteen minutes."

Billy plodded off like a condemned man. Hal stared down at Jen.

"I'm going, too," she said and started to rise.

He held her in place. "I've got plenty of men tonight. I don't need you—and I don't want you there."

She looked up at him in resentment.

"A vice president of MaLaBar sent word about the barge. But your grandfather's behind it. Isn't he?"

She bit her lip and nodded. He crossed his arms and tilted his head slightly, regarding her as if she were a riddle whose answer eluded him. "Why's he playing these games? Why's he bother? He wants you home—but what else?"

She shrugged. He would never understand the situation. Dagobert wanted power, complete power over her. It was that primitive and that simple.

Hal's expression was unyielding. "He's using this situation. You know that, of course."

She nodded. He kept staring at her. "Everybody uses everybody," she murmured at last, echoing Walter Stonebridger.

He nodded cynically. "I thought that's how you'd see it. Even if the whales die, you get your story—and your grandfather gets to play the great savior. MaLaBar Oil gets a star in its crown. I'll hand it to you people—you know how to exploit."

Jen's shame turned to anger. She stood so that she could look him in the eye. Other people were watching them, their attention resting on Jen like a weight, but she didn't care. "If you save those whales, it'll be because of the press and because of MaLaBar Oil," she said, loudly enough for the rest of the room to hear. *Now I've done it,* she thought. *I've stood up in public and taken the enemy's side.*

His mouth slanted bitterly. He looked her up and down. "No. If we save them, it'll be because Billy Owen and Warren Tipana are willing to go out on that ice all night when it's twenty-five below. Otherwise, MaLaBar won't have any whales to rescue."

"Warren?" Jen said, taken aback. "I thought he didn't believe in keeping the whales alive—"

"He believes in keeping his people's good name alive. The world's watching Ultima—and the Inupiat people—thanks to you."

Jen tossed her head, tired of being blamed. "And why are *you* going? I'm sure it's not the 'scientific' thing to do. Are you worried about your reputation, too? Would anybody be going out there tonight if it weren't for the press?"

The corner of his mouth quirked in the same mirthless smile. "Probably not. I'd be stretched out in my bed. But not tonight. I'll be thinking of you curled up in yours instead. A cozy thought for a man on the ice. Sleep well, Miss Martinson."

Jen flushed. For a moment she felt certain that his blue eyes could somehow actually see her warm and naked in her bed. He'd stopped smiling. He turned and left.

Outside the night wind howled and flailed against the windows like a demented thing.

SHE COULDN'T SLEEP. All night the wind screamed and the temperature huddled at a killing twenty-five below. Needles of sleet-like snow rattled at the window pane. She thought of the whales helpless in the storm, their breathing hole being eaten by a growing crust of ice. She thought of Hal and Billy and Warren Tipana fighting the deadly cold to keep the hole open. She thought of what would happen if the barge didn't work. Nothing could open a path to the sea then, and the whales could not be moved from the spot that would become their grave.

She rose at six, dressed and made her way to the deserted dining hall. Alone at a table she sat with her hands folded before her. She would wait here for news of the men. The silence seemed to echo around her.

Arnold arrived at six-thirty, gave her a curt nod and set about making coffee. She went to the door of the kitchen. "Arnold, have you heard anything about Dr. Bailey, Billy, and Mr. Tipana?"

His black eyes cast her a hard glance. He shook his head and went back to his work.

He blames me, Jen thought. Swallowing hard, she returned to her chair. She clasped her hands before her again and stared down at them, her head bowed, her thoughts on Hal. It didn't occur to her that she looked like a woman in troubled prayer.

At ten minutes to seven the door swung open and Hal walked in, limping slightly. His clothing and boots were sodden, and melting ice glinted in the fur of his hood. Cold and wind had darkened his face, and fatigue had etched it. He looked like a man who had battled the ice for a year, not a single night. His eyes met Jen's and narrowed in weary surprise.

He took a cup and filled it with coffee from the metal urn, slowly, as if his hands ached.

Arnold eyed him critically. "Sit. I'll bring you food."

Hal nodded. He took the coffee and sank heavily into the nearest chair. He drained the cup, then set it down and exhaled harshly.

Jen rose, went to him, took his cup and refilled it. She placed it before him and, uninvited, sat down across from him. She studied his face with anxiety. His hair was damp, he needed a shave, and his opened parka was half-soaked.

"Where's Billy? Where's Warren? Are the whales alive? Are they all right? Are you all right? Why are your clothes wet? Shouldn't you change? You're not frostbitten, are you? What happened out there? Were you out there all night long? How cold was it? How long is the storm going to last?"

He took a long drink of coffee. He stared at her, his face stern. Then he smiled. It was more a half smile, only one corner of his mouth turning up, but to Jen it was beautiful. "Too many questions." His voice rasped with fatigue, but the smile stayed. "The whales are okay."

He started to shrug out of his coat. Jen was on her feet, helping him. "This is sopping," she said, hanging it on a nearby chair. "Why? How?"

"The chain saws sprayed ice over us all night. I've had better jobs. Oof." He rubbed his biceps, and Jen noticed that his knuckles were scraped.

She sat down again, taking his hand and examining it. "You're *battered*. And your hand is still cold as ice. Are you sure you're not frostbitten?"

She blew on his fingertips and started chafing his hand, taking care not to touch the hurt knuckles.

Slowly he smiled again. "Careful, Martinson. I could like this. It might be worth sawing ice all night long."

Jen laid his hand back on the table and clasped her own together again. They tingled from touching him. She looked away, embarrassed. "Where's Billy? Is he all right?"

Hal picked up his cup again. "Back in Ultima. He's tired enough to fall in his tracks, but he'll be fine. He's tough."

"The whales are really all right?"

"Your whales are fine, Jen. The breathing hole's still open. They're safe for another day."

She smiled shyly. *You're quite a man,* she wanted to say. *You and Warren and Billy are a breed apart. Not many men would do what you did.* Instead she said, "You need to rest."

"I need to check with Prudhoe Bay about that barge. And the National Guard. And I want some more ice fans flown in. The things work. They stir the water up so it doesn't freeze as fast. But we need more. But if the barge doesn't make it, I don't know what good it'll do. If we could just get them to move on their own—before that ridge of ice thickens any more. It's between them and the open water." He frowned, his mouth grim.

"Hal," she protested, "you can't keep working like this—"

One of the staff, a large man with a black beard, came hurrying in. He gave Jen an unfriendly glance, then eyed Hal with concern. "The lab's already getting calls, Hal. Somebody's on the phone right now from New Zealand. And Tokyo keeps calling."

Hal groaned. "Thanks, Kelpington."

"You're supposed to call Senator Wisner. He's got an important message for you. Likewise the Department of the Interior. One of the high mucky-mucks wants to talk to you."

Hal pushed his chair back and rose. He picked up his sodden parka and slung it over his shoulder. "I'll get on it."

Arnold bustled over, carrying a tray. He set it down, put his hands on his hips and stared at the taller man. "You sit. You eat."

Hal picked up a piece of buttered toast. "I'll eat on the move. Thanks anyway, Arnold." He headed for the door.

"A body needs food," Arnold scolded. "I'm sending a tray to your office, and you *eat*. Then go to bed." He began to mutter in Eskimo. He paused long enough to give Jen one single eloquent accusing look.

HAL NEVER GOT TO BED that day. He stayed on the phone, fielding call after call. He talked to the dozens of experts and advisors that were pouring into the facility. He gave interviews. He kept track of progress of the barge at Prudhoe Bay. At four in the afternoon he called a press conference. He had managed to shave and change his clothes, but he looked haggard from lack of sleep.

"The barge runs," he said. "But it needs repairs. A lot. They've promised to work on it around the clock. The Guard's got a sky crane helicopter waiting to tow it when it's ready."

"Hey! Will it be ready in time?" Over the other voices Jen heard that of Finnegan, the reporter from San Francisco. Since his arrival he had avoided the ice but always pushed to be in the forefront of interviews at the base. Jen didn't like him, and he made her nervous—he always managed to drag Dagobert's name into the proceedings. "Bailey," he shouted again, determined to be heard. "The barge—will it make it in time?"

"I don't know."

"How much longer can the whales hang on?"

"I don't know."

"Are you going to have to work on the ice again tonight?"

"Yes."

"Are you aware that this barge is being sent primarily because of the efforts of one man, Dagobert Martinson, of the Martinson Corporation and one of the major shareholders in MaLaBar?"

Hal's face clouded. "No comment." He glanced briefly at Jen and looked away. It was as if their moment of friendliness at breakfast had never happened.

She waited for him in the hall that evening when he left his office. Weariness shadowed his eyes, but the determination in his face was fierce. Jen knew he was going on willpower, but she also knew the will was iron.

"Are you really going out there again? You haven't slept for thirty-six hours."

He stopped, regarding her coolly. "There's no choice. The storm's stopped, but the temperature's still down. Billy and Warren are going back out. We've got to keep the breathing hole open."

"Why does it have to be you and Billy and Warren? Why not somebody else tonight?"

He shook his head impatiently. "We know how to do it. And nobody else volunteered. Look. Excuse me, I've got to go. We need to get out there before too much ice forms."

She was standing in his path, but she didn't move. Silence fell between them for the length of a heartbeat, then another and another. Her eyes held his as he started to move past her. The movement brought his body within a few inches of hers. Still she didn't budge.

She put her hand on his arm to keep him from moving away. "*I* volunteer," she said.

He stopped, looking as if she'd stung him. *"What?"*

"You said nobody else volunteered. I volunteer. I'm going with you."

"That's ridiculous." He moved her hand from his arm and started to step away.

She reached out and seized his elbow. "I'm strong. I can stand the cold. I stand it better than any of the men reporters. Fifteen minutes on the ice and they're ready to get back to the hotel and a drink. I'm not like that—you know I'm not."

His glance fell to her hand on his sleeve, then traveled back to her eyes. His mouth crooked slightly. "What's the matter? Guilty about your grandfather and MaLaBar trying to be glory hogs?"

"If they can save the whales, they can have the glory. The glory isn't important—saving Goofus and Doofus is. I'm coming with you. If you don't take me, I'll get out there some way—you know I will."

She sensed the growing tautness in his body. Her own was tense. His smile had vanished. "You really think you're something, don't you?"

"No." She set her jaw. "But I can try to become something. You keep saying this is all my fault. All right, maybe it is, but let me help. If you don't take me, I'll hire a cab from Ultima to take me out to the ice and leave me with you. I swear I will. I swear it."

Giving a short, sarcastic laugh, he moved a fraction of an inch closer, as if in challenge. "Rich girls. They always get what they want. You think you want to go out there? You've got a lot to learn. All right. Come out and learn it. You've never been out there at night. It's a killer. You'll quit after five minutes. Spend the whole time shivering in the truck. But if that's what it takes to teach you, fine. Maybe it'll do you some good. Sure. Come on out. You'll find out these aren't the ski slopes of Aspen, sweetheart."

He was mocking her, and she hated it. His nearness was threatening, but she refused to admit the threat or draw back from it. "What if I *can* take it?" she retorted. "Then what?"

His one-cornered smile returned. He looked at the rebellious line of her mouth, the swift rise and fall of her breasts. "If you can take it?" His voice was soft, almost musing. He reached out and took her braid in his hand. He held its silky tip just beneath her chin and caressed its gold smoothness. He brushed it lightly against the curve of her jaw. "Then I could never call you a spoiled brat again, could I? But you wouldn't want that. No. I might start thinking again about undoing your hair, Martinson. And you along with it. You don't want that."

He bent slightly and his lips almost grazed hers. He was so near that she felt as if a bolt of lightning had riven her through. His mouth so near hers seemed to shatter all logical thought, to send waves of delirium dancing through her. She wanted nothing more than for him to kiss her. He did not. He drew back slightly, and once more his smile had faded.

Her body burned, and she was filled with the bewildering sensation of pleasure mixed with alarm. He was so close that her breasts touched the hardness of his chest. His breath was warm against her cheek.

He touched the tip of her braid to her jaw again. He shook his head as if something bothered him deeply, but he said nothing. He drew back farther still. "You really want to go out there?" His voice was low but harsh.

"Yes." She wet her lips.

He watched the movement of the tip of her tongue, his face rigid with control. Slowly he opened his fingers and released her braid, letting it fall.

"Meet me at the motor pool in ten minutes."

He moved away, not touching her again. He strode off without glancing back. He bore himself as if he had already forgotten her and had more important things on his mind.

She stood numbly, watching him go. Raising her hand, she put her fingers against her lips, which tingled as much as if he'd kissed her.

She understood at that moment she would go anywhere, through ice or fire—it didn't matter, as long as he was there, too.

THE SCENE ON THE ICE at night was bizarre, yet magical. The generators hummed, the fans churned, the risen whales sighed and gasped, the water in the breathing hole lapped. The men hooked lights to the generators, and the artificial glare threw strange shadows on the ice and bathed the whales in an eerie yellow glow. In the distance the northern lights stretched and shimmered against the darkness.

The wind was low, which was a blessing, the air crisp and as cold as ice. Jen didn't mind the chill. She was with Hal, and together with Billy and Warren they labored to keep the whales alive in hope that the ice barge would make it.

Every time one of the animals rose, Jen felt a small surge of triumph. They were still alive. They endured.

It proved to be a night of excruciatingly hard work. Yet it was also a night of beauty, for the sky was clear and the aurora borealis glowed particularly bright and played more actively than before.

Hal decided to reopen one of the two old breathing holes the whales had refused to use. He wanted to try joining it to the active one, giving the whales substantially more room. He'd set two of the new ice fans in thick slush that had formed in the nearest breathing hole and turned them on.

At first he refused to let Jen use a saw, although she said she had often helped her grandfather saw wood at his place on Big Sur. But Warren Tipana eyed her shrewdly, then spoke in Eskimo, which Billy translated. Let the woman try, Warren had said. The Eskimos knew women had great powers of endurance, and this woman was young and tall and when she moved, she did it as smoothly as a seal in the water. Her body served her well.

Grudgingly Hal let her try, and even more grudgingly admitted she seemed equal to the task. After the first two hours, as work grew more intense, his distrust faded. He seemed to accept her, even to value her help, and she felt proud, as if she had become part of an elite team.

Now, by his side, she was cold, wet and tired, but she also felt oddly happy. She smiled at him and thought he smiled back. Although her arms ached, she kept working, determined to do her part.

There in the cold and the vastness they were playing out a drama against enormous odds. Darkness arched over their little island of artificial light, and in the distance the ancient natural lights of the north danced their silent ballet.

Jen's blood began to course with strange excitement. Exhausting as cutting the ice and pushing it out of the way was, she was exhilarated. It was wonderful to be in such a mysterious night, and it was wonderful to be doing something at last to help the whales. It seemed right to be beside Hal, to give every ounce of her strength to help him.

Sometime just before midnight, when he took a short break to change the broken chain on his saw, she stopped, too, to catch her breath and change her gloves.

"Go back to the truck. Rest. You've done enough for one night," he told her. His voice was gruff.

"No. I didn't come to rest. I came to help."

She watched him, his face shadowy beneath the furred hood. He didn't look at her. Instead he stared up at the stars, which were preternaturally bright. "I said you've done enough. Go on. That's an order."

A wave of loneliness engulfed her. Perhaps he did not accept her after all. But she knew she could keep on working—she could do it all night if she had to. "You should know by now that I don't take orders very well."

He kept staring at the stars. "I should know a lot of things by now. I should have known you'd throw yourself into this, heart first. I should know that when you start something you never quit. You're going to kill yourself if you keep this up. I don't want you—"

"I'm fine," she objected. "I'm probably better off than you. I didn't spend last night out here. I didn't fight off the press all day."

He shook his head, then looked at her. He shook his head again. She could just make out his face in the darkness, and the look in his eyes made her forget the cold, the huge and eerie silence, even her fatigue. Her heart began to hammer erratically.

"You're impossible." His low voice was intent. "Do you know that? You're impossible—everything about you. Sometimes all I want is for you to go away. And other times, what I want most is—"

"Holy—! Oh, good grief, *good grief*!" It was Billy's voice, and he was screaming with excitement. "Hal! Come here! Come *here*!"

"What—" Hal spun to look across the ice. So did Jen. She blinked uncomprehendingly at the lights surrounding the second breathing hole. It took a moment for what she saw to sink in.

A miracle had occurred.

The second breathing hole had almost been restored to its original size, and the fans had churned it almost free of ice.

But the hole was no longer empty. A huge shape loomed there, glistening in the artificial light. Goofus had moved.

His huge snout pointed at the stars while he rasped for breath. Jen could not believe it. Hal had said the whales had ignored the new breathing holes for over a week before she had come. The animals had resisted every effort, every lure to make them move. That was why they were at the mercy of the ice and their only hope had been the barge from MaLaBar. But now Goofus had moved, of his own volition.

Suddenly the situation no longer seemed so desperate. Jen's heart went winging like a bird.

Before she could fully realize what was happening, the water churned and splattered again, startling her even more. Doofus, too, appeared, shooting his triangle of spray.

Billy gave a whoop of exultation, and Warren Tipana grinned from ear to ear. Jen turned in wonder to Hal, who took her in his arms so tightly she gasped. He, too, grinned—a wide, lop-sided smile of disbelief. "They moved on their own—" He laughed. "We may have a fighting chance after all—even if the barge never makes it. My God."

He hugged her close and she hugged him back. "I'll be..." he muttered in amazement. "I'll be...." He picked her up and whirled her around. She laughed in delight.

"I think they came to the lights," Billy yelled. He laughed, too, with pleased surprise. "Or the sound of the fans. Or both. Do you know what this means?"

Hal kept Jen locked securely in his arms. He grinned even more widely. "We can lead them to the sea. If we have time to get them past that pressure ridge that's forming. That's something. It's the first real progress we've made. My God, who ever knew a whale would come to light? Who'd have thought it?"

He squeezed Jen again, and she hugged him back. She resisted the desire to kiss him for pure joy.

He looked at her, suddenly conscious of what he was doing. He released her immediately.

Suddenly the night seemed twice as chill to Jen. His embrace had ended so suddenly that it pained her far more than the cold. But the ghost of a smile stayed on her face. The whales had moved. It was a miracle, a small one. But it might be enough.

"We may not have to depend on the barge, after all," Billy yelled. "Maybe we've got a prayer, even without it."

"We'll see," Hal said. "Come on, Big Bill, let's open up that third breathing hole. If they'll come to that, we'll know we've really got a chance."

The night became a blur for Jen, of darkness, cold and flying flakes of sawn ice, of the aurora shimmering and the shine of brilliant stars. Of bone-numbing weariness mixed with the intoxication of hope. They worked feverishly now, taking turns sawing and pushing aside the cut ice.

At first Hal tried to make Jen rest, but she refused so firmly that he stopped asking. She worked at his side, resolved to last as long as the men did.

By four o'clock in the morning, they were all nearing collapse from cold and weariness. But they were rewarded when first Goofus, then Doofus, surfaced in the third breathing space, once more drawn by the lights and the sound of the fans. When the whales appeared there,

Jen, half-drunk with fatigue, thought she had never seen anything so beautiful as those two barnacled snouts shining in the starlight. She wanted to weep with happiness and relief.

She stretched out on the ice and reached to Goofus. When he came to her mittened hand for a welcoming caress, she did weep. But her tears started to freeze, and she had to scrub at them like a child. "You're going to be all right," she told Goofus, wiping the tears. "We can save you now."

Hal watched her. He bent and hauled her gently to her feet. "Come on," he said. "Don't get your hopes too high. We've worked enough for one night. Let's go home."

Billy and Warren drove their snow machines back to Ultima. Jen rode in the truck with Hal. They returned to the base in silence, exhaustion mixed with exhilaration.

For the first time since they'd found the whales trapped, Hal had a cautious sense of hope. The main problem would be the pressure ridge forming between the whales and open water. If it thickened to more than a few feet, saws could not cut it, and even the barge could not pierce it. But with luck—a great deal—the whales just might make it back to the sea. And the woman beside him...he did not want to think of the woman beside him.

She had been like a part of him tonight. Out on the ice all differences between them had fallen away. She had worked without complaint and with all her heart. He could only marvel at her. No, he tried not to think about her and what had happened between them out there, not yet.

Next to him, Jen, her euphoria nearly worn away, felt dazed. She watched the aurora borealis. Its lights had danced north and were beginning to fade. All she wanted was to lean against Hal's shoulder. But that would be like begging for his affection, so she did nothing.

Hal parked the truck and wordlessly unloaded it. But then, still not speaking, he wound his arm around Jen and led her into the facility. She allowed herself at last to lean against him as he guided her through the hallways. He opened the door to his apartment and, saying nothing, ushered her inside.

She didn't question it when he closed the door behind them and turned on a small lamp. He stepped toward her and unfastened her parka, hanging it over the back of a chair. Then he began on the flannel shirt she wore over her sweater. When he had undone all the buttons, he stopped and looked into her eyes.

He took a deep, harsh breath. He stepped away, went into his bedroom and returned with a white terry robe. "Here." Once more his voice was gruff. "Take a shower and put this on. I'll fix you a drink."

She nodded and didn't allow herself to question the rightness of being in his rooms. She simply did as he said. When she returned to the living room, feeling rosy and tingling from the shower, he stood by the couch. He wore a dry pair of jeans and no shirt. The corded muscles of his bare arms gleamed in the lamplight.

Jen was bundled in his robe, which was too large. She walked to his side. She trembled slightly.

"Here," he said, handing her a glass. "Sit. Drink."

She sat and so did he, his arm around her shoulders. He raised his glass and drank. She did likewise. He set his glass on the coffee table. So did she.

He leaned closer and reached for her braid. He kissed her for a long, delirious moment.

Then he drew back and looked into her eyes.
"Now," he said.
And he began to unbraid her hair.

CHAPTER TEN

SHE WAS IN HIS ARMS and in his bed, languorous with weariness and desire. He embraced her, and the warmth embraced them both. Lamplight from the living room fell through the door, illuminating the bedroom faintly.

She snuggled against the heat of his bare chest. The starched sheets crackled as he shifted his body so that he lay propped on one elbow beside her, leaning over her. One hand pushed aside the robe to rest on the bared skin of her shoulder, the other played in the freed wealth of her hair. Her hair, unbound, was slightly damp from the shower, and he wound it around his fingers and spread it like a gold cape across her naked shoulder and his own.

He bent and kissed her behind the ear, then on the curve of her neck where it met her shoulder. His lips moved to the silky hollow of her throat, then to the line of her jaw, precisely where her pulse throbbed. He kissed the corner of her mouth. At last his lips met hers.

She sighed happily as she tasted the desire and sweetness of his touch. She put one hand on the warm column of his neck. Beneath her fingers his pulse jumped just as erratically as hers. Her other hand found his, and they stretched their arms out together, their fingers intertwined.

Her robe fell open further, and his lips traveled downward until he was kissing her between the breasts. She heard his long and ragged sigh, felt its warmth against her flesh.

He raised his face so it was even with hers. He disengaged his hand from hers and stroked her hair again. Slowly, with great deliberation, he lowered his mouth to hers once more. His lips were weather-roughened but hot against her own.

He touched one hand to her face, his thumb light against the pulse that leaped to sudden life in her jaw. She felt his other hand slip beneath the robe and settle restlessly on the satiny small of her back. His touch electrified her. She clung to him, feeling half-faint with love for him.

He'd awakened such dizzying warm tides of emotion in her with simply a kiss that she felt she already belonged to him. She was his, his alone, and she had been, she knew, from her first night in Ultima. She believed he felt the same as she did, swept away by love and tenderness. They had both struggled against the pull of their desires too long. She could fight no further.

She wound her arms around his neck and buried her face against the heat of his throat. "I love you," she said.

"Hush," he said softly, his hand moving back to bury itself in her loosened hair. He brought his lips next to hers again.

"I do," she murmured. "I love you."

"Hush," he said again and smoothed her hair. "You don't know what you're saying. You're exhausted."

She pressed her face closer to him, settled nearer. "I do love you," she repeated. "Do you feel the same way? You have to."

"Hush. . . ." He pulled her closer, holding her against him so that she couldn't move away. She felt secure in his arms and whole. He pressed his face against her hair but didn't kiss her again.

She loved him, she thought, and he loved her. She nestled beside him happily. Surely he loved her, or he couldn't look at her so, touch her so. He could not hold her so possessively if he didn't love her.

Yet the arms around her were taut with restraint, and his hands no longer moved so deliciously over her body that she felt faint with pleasure. He propped himself on his elbow and stared into her eyes. Even in the semidarkness she could tell how intent his gaze was. "Jen," he said. "Jennifer. Jennie."

"I want to touch you. I want you to kiss me," she told him.

"You're too tired to know what you want." His voice was strained. "Don't talk about love. You and I have no business talking about love."

The words hurt, but, reckless, she ignored them. "Then we won't talk. Oh, Hal, just hold me, please. Don't let me go."

"Hold you? Jennie, I'd hold you for the rest of my life, but—"

"But what?" Her arm tightened around his neck as his gaze moved over her. Some inner conflict played on the shadows of his angular face.

His fingertips drew near her cheek, nearly touched it, but did not. They hovered there a moment, then moved away. They found the lapel of the opened robe and pulled it across her breast, covering her again. "I've got no business having you in my bed."

"I want to be in your bed."

"Neither of us knows what we're doing." He shook his head. "I haven't slept for forty-eight hours. And you're exhausted. You shouldn't be here."

"Please," she breathed, inhaling his closeness, his warmth. "Let me stay. Don't send me away."

He gave a long, ragged sigh and fell back on the pillow, his arm still coiled around her shoulders. "We can't make love—it'd be crazy." He gave a bitter laugh. "It wouldn't even be good—a fast, exhausted fumble." He shook his head again, and the starched pillow crackled softly. "You and I? It'd be the mistake of the century."

"It's not a mistake. It can't be. I lo—"

He put his fingertips against her lips, silencing her. "Don't. You don't know what you're saying. Stop it, Jen."

"I want to stay with you. Here."

He drew one hand along her face, his fingers tracing first the curve of her cheekbone, then the line of her jaw. He was silent for a long moment. His hand settled on her shoulder, and she could feel the restraint in his touch. "I'll hold you, Jen. That's all. Rest, sweetheart. Sleep. You need it."

I need you, she wanted to cry, but bit back the words. She had shamed herself, telling him she wanted him. He didn't love her. He was merely tired and needed human warmth.

It was good, she supposed, that he was strong enough to think of what was foolish and what wasn't. She had been past such considerations. But if, for some reason, he didn't want to let her go, she could not bring herself to leave him, either.

She let him draw her close to him again, pressed her cheek once more against his chest. He held her tight in his arms. But he made no other movement to touch her.

She lay, tensed, savoring his nearness, wondering if she meant anything at all to him. Perhaps he himself didn't know. He had gone without sleep too long, worked too hard, been through too much in the last forty-eight hours.

Soon the steady rise and fall of his chest told her that sleep had at last claimed him. Sometimes his arm twitched slightly and his fingers stirred restlessly against her shoulder, as if his muscles were still rebelling against what he had put them through.

Jen sighed, spent by the long night's work and her own emotions. She closed her eyes and nestled against him, secure in the fortress of his arms.

She slept at last.

SHE AWOKE in his bed, deliciously warm and sleepy. She still wore his white robe, and for a moment she imagined that her face still lay against his chest and that she could feel the strong beat of his heart beneath her cheek, feel the hard warmth of his muscles.

Her long hair spilled in a golden tangle over the pillows, both hers and his. She remembered his hands, warm and gentle, moving through it. Looking at his side of the bed, she realized it was empty. She blinked in confusion.

She was alone. He had already left her. She sat up, pushing her hair back. She looked at her watch. It was ten o'clock in the morning. The apartment echoed with emptiness.

What happened? she thought, bewildered. *And where is he?* Unconsciously, she picked up his pillow, hugging it to her. She wanted him stretched out next to her, lean and wind-burnished, his brown hair tousled with sleep. She wanted to look down and see his face, shadowed by a day's growth of beard, see his lashes casting sharp shadows on his cheekbones.

I love him, she thought in panic. *And I told him so.* She'd fallen into bed with him last night without asking any questions. She would have done anything for him, and he must have known it.

But they had done nothing. Not really, she thought in confusion. He'd held her, kissed her, nothing more. He had drawn back from her at the last minute, and she knew why. It was because she had told him she loved him, not once but three times.

She pulled the lapels of the robe together more tightly, her cheeks flaming. She was deeply shamed by the emotion she'd shown. He hadn't wanted that much involvement and had tried to protect both of them from her folly.

She had gone to bed thinking she was filled with deathless passion. He, on the other hand, had been feeling merely... a bit friendly.

She fell back against the pillow, feeling foolish and hollow. He hadn't said he loved her. He hadn't so much as said he'd liked her. And when morning came, without a word, he'd left her here, alone.

I'll tell him I was tired, that's all, she thought. *I'll tell him it was just craziness talking, just fatigue.*

Feeling empty and shaky, she went next door to Keenan's apartment, dressed, then brushed and braided her hair. She called the Redwood City *Sentinel* and left her story with an office boy who was holding down the rewrite desk for some reason that Jen couldn't understand. The connection was bad, and the boy kept saying, "What? What?"

She hung up, hoping he'd understood that the story was important. They had learned something of great importance about whales last night. Now that the animals would move on their own, swimming toward light and familiar sound, they had two chances at freedom instead of one. Both might be slim, but they were something.

She squared her shoulders. She had to find Hal and try to explain that last night had been a mistake. If he felt her love was a burden, she would lift it from him. It was the least she could do, and perhaps it would leave her with a scrap of pride. But still, as she remembered lying in his strong, bare arms, she was overcome with yearning for him, for his face, his touch, the feel of his mouth upon her own. She loved him. She must tell him she did not.

AS SOON AS SHE NEARED the dining hall, she knew that something was wrong. A tenseness seemed to sharpen the air, and as she approached, she heard an uneasy undercurrent of voices.

Two men came bolting out of the dining hall, almost running. One of them was a television cameraman, and he ran into her, almost dropping his Minicam. He dodged around her, trying to catch up with the other man, who also carried a camera.

"What—?" Jen cried, rubbing her shoulder, for the man had hit her forcefully enough to hurt.

"Sorry, blondie," the second cameraman called over his shoulder. "We got a chance to snag a flight to Prudhoe."

Prudhoe, thought Jen. Why were television people going to Prudhoe Bay?

"What's wrong?" she called after them, but neither answered. She increased her pace and hurried into the dining hall, which was crowded. There were more people than there'd been the day before, she thought, a sick feeling settling around her heart. Another dozen or so must have come in on the morning flight.

She looked for Billy but couldn't find him. At last she saw Finnegan, the reporter from San Francisco, and made her way toward him. "What's happening?" she asked.

Finnegan sat at a table, a cup of coffee at his elbow as he scribbled in a notebook. He glanced up. "If it isn't the heiress. You're late this morning. Where've you been? Or would you rather not say?"

His wrinkled face rearranged itself into something resembling a smile, and he waggled his eyebrows at her as if he and she shared a dirty secret.

He knows Hal and I spent the night together, she thought in panic. And that meant Dagobert would find out. If he didn't know already.

She pulled her attention away from her own problems. "Something's going on around here. What?"

"Why should I tell you?" He stood, shrugged and gave her one of his insinuating grins again. "But then why not? I called my story in two hours ago. While you were still snug in your bed. Or somebody's."

She resisted the urge to slap him as hard as she could. She didn't know how he had found out, but the pleased gleam in his eye told her that it was his business to know such things.

"Tell me what's happening," she demanded.

He glanced around the room with maddening nonchalance. "It looks as if your boyfriend has to get those whales to open water all by himself. The MaLaBar barge is burning."

Jen's mouth fell open. She stared at Finnegan in disbelief. *"What?"*

"Your whale story gets more expensive by the hour, sweety. I said the barge is burning. If they don't get the fire put out soon, the hoverbarge'll be at the bottom of the sea. A million dollars in machinery lost. All for a couple of animals too stupid to head south when they should have."

He started to walk away, but Jen seized him by the sleeve of his baggy sweater. "Was anybody hurt?"

He laughed. "No. Too bad. It would have been a better story. It's just the barge that's lost. It almost pulled a two-million-dollar helicopter out of the sky, too, but didn't. More's the pity. What a story that would have been."

He tried to step away again, but Jen refused to let him. "Where's Hal Bailey?"

"Out on the ice, sugar. See, you've put him in a hell of a position. He's scraped up a rescue team. But can they beat the odds? I doubt it. In fact I'm taking bets. Care to lay a little wager? Take my advice—the safe money says the whales won't make it. Too bad. But then we can all go home. Including you."

Jen released his sleeve as if it were poisoned. "You're really something, Finnegan."

He lit a cigarette and tossed the match in an ashtray. "I'm a reporter. You're a rich kid playing games. You start a story rolling for the fun of it. It costs MaLaBar—and your grandfather—a cool million. It almost costs the National Guard two million. It turns this base and this town upside down. It disrupts everybody's life, including mine. But what do you care? You're playing."

"I'm not *playing*," she said, her teeth clenched.

"No?" He took a long drag from his cigarette. "Playing—and playing around. One boyfriend dumps you, so you pick up another one. You've used Bailey, just like you've used your grandfather's influence to keep this story going. Well, now lover boy's out there on that ice—

and he's your story. I hope he doesn't kill himself for it. But if he does, I hope you were worth it."

Finnegan walked away, the cigarette clamped between his lips, a crooked smirk on his face. Jen stared after him, breathing hard. She wanted to get to a phone, to call Billy, beg him to come to the base and take her out on the ice where Hal was.

Someone tapped her on the shoulder. She whirled and saw Kelpington, the black-bearded meteorologist. "Kelpington—is it true? The barge is burning?"

"It's true." His face was no friendlier than ever.

"How about the weather?"

His expression grew grimmer still. "Bad. We're in for a series of storms. Listen, there's a call for you in my office. I don't like having my phone tied up with personal calls, but—"

"Lead the way," she said, tossing her head.

Kelpington's disapproval was the least of her problems. She followed him through the maze of halls.

He ushered her into his cluttered office, then closed the door so that she might have some privacy. "Hello?"

Just as she suspected, the voice on the other end of the wire was Dagobert's. It was an angry voice. "Where have you been? Finnegan says you spent the night with that Bailey SOB—did you? I won't have it, do you hear?"

Her heart shriveled. "We worked until after four in the morning. I fell asleep at his place, that's all. Nothing happened."

She took a deep breath and held it. What she said was the truth, even if it wasn't all of it.

"If I *ever* find out that man's touched you, he can kiss his career goodbye. Do you hear me? He'll never work again—I'll see to it."

"Nothing happened," Jen insisted, finding refuge again in partial truth.

"I raised you to be a princess. You're a woman fit for royalty. You're not going to waste yourself on some—some scoundrel who snoops in the seaweed."

"Keenan snoops in seaweed," she countered.

"Keenan's going to inherit forty million dollars. He can afford to do whatever he likes, and he's an idiot anyway. This Bailey man is not good enough for you. I don't like him, he's defied me, and now he's using you to get to me, and if he so much as touches you, I'll destroy him—destroy him. *Do you understand me?*"

She let out her breath. Once more she felt trapped, cornered. "I understand," she said.

"How do you like the way your story's going?" Dagobert went on. "Are you satisfied now? Eh?"

She was sitting at Kelpington's desk, staring at a crystal globe paperweight that seemed to snow inside when shaken. "No, Dagobert. I'm not happy. I heard the barge is on fire."

"I could have told you the fool thing would never work," he snapped. "We're lucky it didn't pull the 'copter out of the sky so that MaLaBar would have to pay for *that*, too. Now how do you expect to free those silly whales?"

A smothering sensation grew in her chest. "The men will try to do it alone."

"They'll never make it. More bad weather's on the way. They can work themselves to death and they'll never make it."

Tears burned her eyes. "They can try."

"Try? Try? A real man *does*. You want those whales free, you talk to *me*. You ask *me*."

She picked up Kelpington's paperweight. She turned it so that the glittering artificial snow swirled. A tear spilled over and ran down her cheek. "And how could you save them? The barge is burning, Dagobert. You're as helpless as anybody else now. The men here are the only hope."

"I've never been helpless. Ask me for help. Just ask."

"There's nothing you can do."

"Are you crying? Jennifer Anne, are you crying? Now don't feel bad. You come home to Grandpa. He'll fix everything, just like always. He's the one who loves you best." The voice was low, gentle, the way she remembered him sounding from happier times.

"I'm sorry, Dagobert," she said, scrubbing away the futile tears. "I just—can't talk. And I've got to get out on the ice—"

"Are you going to *him*? Jen, honey, don't. Trust me. It could never work. You're too different. Money makes you different. He'd either use you for it or hate you for it. A man like that can't have you. And you can't have him. He'd resent everything you stand for."

The weight on her chest seemed intolerable now. Dagobert, with his flawless instincts, had zeroed in on the most painful truths. He always did.

She watched the last of the snow settle in the paperweight. "He doesn't care about me, Dagobert. He just cares about his work. And Alaska. I know he'd never be interested in me. If only because of what you're going to do to Bristol Bay—"

"Bristol Bay? He's worried about my drilling in Bristol Bay? He is, is he? Listen, precious—"

Jen felt too torn to go on. "Dagobert, I can't talk anymore. I'm sorry about the barge. I really am. Goodbye."

For the first time in her life she hung up on him. She sat with her head in her hands. Suddenly she no longer wanted to be a reporter. She didn't know what she wanted.

She thought of lying in Hal's arms and wished nothing more than to be there again. But he had turned from her when she'd said she loved him. And she couldn't blame him. What Dagobert had said was all too true. A man like Hal could not love a woman like her. It was impossible. Her whole life was impossible.

Stop feeling sorry for yourself, she said furiously. *If you quit this, you'll never finish anything as long as you live. Get hold of yourself.* She straightened up, dug in her purse for a handkerchief and dried her eyes.

She picked up the receiver and dialed Billy's number. Her job, like Hal's, was out on the ice.

THE SCENE AT THE ICE approached bedlam. A team of Eskimo men, led by Warren Tipana and Hal, cut new holes in the ice. The snarl of chain saws filled the air.

The ice, once clean and clear, was disfigured by the dirty tracks of dozens of vehicles. It swarmed with people. A photographer from a major magazine was being led back to a car, his hands seriously frostbitten. A helicopter clattered overhead.

A great many officials, who had come from a great many far-flung agencies, milled about looking dazed. They had been dispatched by their various bureaus. Now they shivered and danced in the cold, looking bewildered about precisely what they were supposed to do.

A few of the men with the most impressive titles were making statements to anyone who would listen. Jen and Billy watched from the parked truck. "Jeez," Billy said in disgust, "look at the whales. They look terrible."

Jen studied the creatures with rising concern. They looked more tired than ever—if that were possible—not rising quite so high to draw their breaths. The unnatural flurry of activity around them seemed to make them anxious.

She searched the crowd for Hal, and her heart gave a jolting leap when she saw him. He was, of course, working beside Warren Tipana, his face taut with strain as he and Warren and another man struggled to push a huge block of cut ice beneath the lip of fast ice at the edge of the hole.

"How does he do it?" she breathed.

Billy didn't ask whom she meant. He gave a wry, slight smile and shook his head as Jen turned her eyes back to Hal. "I don't know." His smile faded. "But I should be helping, too. It's up to us to save them now. Nobody else can."

"Billy, let me help, too," she said.

He shook his head. "No. See if you can get Hal to take a break. He needs it."

He climbed out of the truck, and she watched as he made his way to where the men were struggling to open a new breathing hole.

Hal looked harried and bone tired. He also looked determined to work until he dropped. He and Warren were putting all their muscle into the job of shoving the heavy ice chunks out of the way.

She descended from the truck and made her way among the crowd to where he labored. Sweat glistened on his brow and dampened his hair. With a pained grunt, he heaved his force against the ice, and Warren did the same. The huge slab slipped under the fast ice at the edge of the breathing hole, disposed of at last.

She laid her mittened hand on his arm. "How long have you been out here?" It was eleven and the sun was up, hanging low in the south.

He wiped his brow. "A couple of hours."

"How many hours did you work yesterday?" She studied the fatigue on his face and wished she could kiss it away.

"I don't know. Sixteen, seventeen."

"And the day before?" she probed, her hand still on his arm.

"A little more maybe. Look, I've got to get back to this. The barge is burning, Jen. We've got to try to make it alone."

"Hal," she pleaded, "take a break. Please. Billy can take over for you for a while. We've got coffee in the truck."

He looked into her eyes and saw the worry. "All right," he finally said, surprising her. "Five minutes."

They crossed the ice and climbed into the truck. He let her pour him a cup of coffee. He stripped off his gloves and glove liners to feel the warmth of the hot cup against his hands. He bent his head and took a deep drink.

"I'm sorry about the barge," she said. "I'm just glad nobody got hurt."

He stared out at the swarms of people moving aimlessly on the ice, getting in the way of the Eskimo workers. "I never had much faith in it. I don't know if they could ever have got it out of Prudhoe Bay. The helicopter could barely move it."

She put her hand over one of his. He let it stay. "What about the pressure ridge of ice? Can you cut through it?"

He shook his head. "I don't know, Jen. I just don't know. It's growing. It's getting wider and deeper. It might already be too much for chain saws. We'll have to get out there with axes. I don't know if it can be done. All we can do is try. The whales are still weakening. I give them another four days if they can't get to open water. Five at the most."

They sat a moment in silence. He kept staring at the ice, at the people cluttering it. "That's a good crew out there, Jen. They're men of iron, they truly are. They've got four new holes open already. They've got the whales closer to the sea in three hours than MaLaBar has in the last twenty-four. But it might not be enough."

He picked up her hand and squeezed it. His own was roughened by cold and hard with calluses. "We might not make it. I'm sorry. We'll do all we can."

She let her fingers twine with his. "I know."

"This—" he gestured at the figures darkening the ice, most of them milling without purpose "—this is out of hand. The world seems to think this is a fairy tale and will have a happy ending. I don't think it can. A lot of people will be disappointed. I'm sorry about that, too."

She could think of no reply. He exhaled, a sound of exasperation. He squeezed her hand again. "What happened last night—between you and me—won't happen again. I'm sorry about that, too. Being out on the ice that long, it's sort of like getting drunk on fatigue. A man does stupid things."

The words hurt. But he kept her hand in his, as if he felt some sort of reluctant affection for her. "I'm the stupid one," she murmured. Bitterness and sorrow tinged her words.

He looked into her eyes, his own guarded. "I..." He fell silent.

She stared at him, her heart beating so hard it hurt.

"I thought about us," he said. "About you and me. It doesn't take much thinking to know it wouldn't work. You know that."

He squeezed her hand one last time, then let it go. "It's like we come from opposite ends of the earth." He reached out to adjust the folds of her muffler.

Jen bit the inside of her lower lip. She tried not to flinch, not to show any emotion. She knew what he meant. He could not be involved with a member of the Martinson family. His conscience would not allow it. The Martinson Corporation stood for everything he opposed. It was the enemy, and she was part of it. She was its offspring.

She nodded, as if she understood and accepted what he said. He put his arm along the back of the seat. "I've got a guy coming from the Department of the Interior. I'll have to put him up with me. The hotel's already got four people to a room. I may have to put some of the women that are coming in your place. So I won't have much chance to see you alone again before all this is over."

Before all this is over. Her heart seemed to fall into some dark abyss. In four or five days the story would end, one way or another, and he was telling her goodbye.

He toyed a bit more with her scarf, then drew back his hand. "You're going to be a very rich lady some day. Just look back and remember that there's a biologist up in the Arctic or out in the Pacific someplace who..."

He paused again, unable to find words. He looked away from her. "Who wishes you well," he finished.

Outwardly she remained calm. She swallowed, trying to get rid of the knot in her throat. "I said some foolish things last night. I didn't mean them."

He kept looking out at the crowd on the ice. "Consider it all forgotten."

She nodded numbly. She tried again to swallow and couldn't. "Do you think they're doomed—the whales? Honestly?"

He looked at her, blue eyes as steady as ever. "Another squall's coming. It's going to be hell out here. What we need is an ice-breaking ship. We need it now, and it's impossible to get one."

She was humiliated to realize she was crying again. She brushed away her tears, angry that he had witnessed her weakness.

He reached out to adjust her scarf again but stopped himself. "Jen," he told her, "I'll do everything in my power to save them. I promise you that. I just can't promise success."

She watched the smaller whale rise, bobbing and showing its face, patched with cuts and splotches of frostbite. She knew Hal spoke the truth. He had committed himself to saving them, and he'd die trying if that's what it took.

He breathed deeply. He set his emptied cup on the dashboard. "I've got to get back out there," he said. "Look. I've misjudged you. I've given you a rough time up here. And this—" he looked out at the ice, his expression grim "—this is pretty crazy. But I want to tell you, you're not a bad kid. In fact, you're pretty special."

To her surprise he leaned across the seat and kissed her. It was a brief kiss, almost brotherly, and it ended far too soon. Before she realized what was happening, he was out the door and heading back toward the work crew with long strides. She touched her fingertips to her lips and stared after him. She realized what had happened. He had just kissed her goodbye.

THAT NIGHT another storm smashed into the north slope. Hal and a crew of men from Ultima worked most of the night, and Warren Tipana collapsed from exhaustion. He was taken to the doctor in Ultima, who told him to rest for at least a week.

Jen, now sharing her apartment with a woman from the Fisheries Bureau, heard Hal come in sometime after five in the morning. He was back on the ice again by noon the next day. This time the storm was holding, howling like a pack of demons, and no reporters or officials braved it. Billy, who was working long hours beside Hal, could not be spared to take her. She would have joined them, but they had a large crew of men now. She could not hope to keep up with them or really help.

Like the other reporters, she waited, drinking countless cups of coffee, with no news to call in except the same story: Eskimo Crew Braves Elements as Time Runs Short. Whales Weaken.

Hal came in that afternoon to try to sleep before the night's work. There were too many calls awaiting him, too many questions to be answered, too many decisions to be made. He ended up holding an impromptu press conference in the lounge, and Jen was frightened at how tired he looked.

Once more he worked most of the night. At morning, the storm still held. If anything its fury had increased. She bribed a highly reluctant Arnold to drive her out to where the men were working.

The wind increased, even as they drove. Arnold parked the truck, and she got out, holding her arm before her eyes to make her way through the blinding snow. She could barely see, and the men working on the ice were only gray shapes.

When Hal recognized her, he straightened up from his chain saw, laid it aside and came to her. "What are you doing here?" he demanded. He had to shout to be heard over the wind. "Get back to base, Jen. There's nothing you can do here."

She squinted against the lash of the driving snow. The cold was so intense it was painful, but the sight of Hal filled her with such alarm she forgot the cold. Ice coated his parka, thickly crusted the fur of his hood. His boots were stiff with ice, his gloves like pieces of armor. His eyebrows, even his lashes were white with it, his face gray with cold.

"Hal—" she said, but could say nothing else. He was naturally lean, but now he looked gaunt. He must have lost ten pounds in the last two days. His lips were cracked from the cold. "Oh, Hal."

"Jenny, time's running out. I can't stop. Go back. I can't take time for you."

The whales rose in a nearby breathing hole. Their appearance alarmed her as much as Hal's did. The smaller whale was starting to look somehow withered, his snout gray from frostbite. The larger was more badly scraped than ever.

She tried to see out to the open water. She couldn't. The man hadn't made it halfway yet. She suddenly realized they weren't going to make it in time unless a miracle occurred. "Hal, you've got to rest."

"Jennie, honey, we can't rest. We've got to keep going. If we don't get them past that ridge by tomorrow night, it can't be done. It's all over."

"You don't even know if you can make it past the ridge now—you may all be killing yourselves for nothing. It may be hopeless—"

He took her by the arms and peered into her face. His own was so drawn with fatigue it looked like a stranger's. "We started this. We have to see it through. What would people think of Ultima and its people if we quit? You of all people should understand. Go back. There's nothing you can do."

She stared at him hopelessly. He looked at her and shook his head. "Jennie," he said again.

He released her and was gone. He had rejoined the men. Jen looked at their shadowy figures with a lump in her throat. She turned and fled back to the truck.

THAT EVENING Jen could not eat. She didn't go to the dining hall. She sat alone in Keenan's apartment, thinking of the men on the ice, how brutal conditions were, yet how they kept going, hopeless as the situation seemed.

The phone rang. She picked it up with shaking fingers. She hadn't talked to Dagobert for two days and hoped it wasn't he. It was.

"It doesn't look like Bailey's going to make it," he said with obvious satisfaction.

The bitterness in her voice surprised her. "Did you just call to gloat?"

"No. I called up to bring my girl back home. Start packing."

She closed her eyes and began to massage her forehead. "Dagobert, I'm tired unto death of your games. I'm not leaving until—until this is over."

"Really?" He feigned surprise. "Would you leave to save your precious whales?"

Her hand went still. She opened her eyes. "What do you mean? The barge is ruined. It's a floating wreck."

"Apparently it was always a floating wreck. A colossal maritime mistake. No—I'm talking about real help. What if I can get a real ship there—a Soviet ice cutter?"

Jen had the odd sensation that she had frozen. She could not move, she could not blink, she could not even feel.

Dagobert paused, letting his question sink in. "What if," he amended, "we say I *have* a Soviet ice cutter in position to get there fast? And that with a few phone calls, I can have the government give it emergency clearance to get into our waters, to get directly to Ultima, in fact? No waiting period. What if we say I could have it there by tomorrow morning? What would we say to our granddaddy then? Hmm, miss?"

She inhaled deeply, testing to see if she could still breathe. She thought of the whales, their strength draining away as the storm closed in. She thought of the men fighting the ice and snow to save them, and how long both men and animals suffered in vain. She thought of Hal, sleepless, ice freezing to his flesh. She thought of the miracle they needed. She found her voice. It was choked. "You can do it?"

Dagobert let a beat of silence skip by. "I can. I've called in every favor ever owed me and promised more than I called in. But I can do it. Just ask. Just say 'please.'"

She still felt as if she had been turned to ice or stone. What would it matter now if she asked for his help? He was the only chance for the whales' survival. Hal did not want her there, and she had fallen out of love with reporting—all the job had allowed her to do was reap the whirlwind, a harvest of confusion and emptiness.

Dagobert took her silence for reluctance. "I don't want you near that Bailey man. He's not good enough for you.

He'd turn you against me. But I'll tell you what. I'll let you give him a goodbye present."

She blinked. "A goodbye present?" she asked dully.

"Come home, and I'll not only send the ice cutter, I'll stay out of Bristol Bay. How's that? Now which do you think Bailey would rather have? You—when he knows he could never make you happy? Or for me to give up my interests in Bristol Bay? Hmm?"

She felt more stunned than before. "You'd stay out of Bristol Bay? You wouldn't drill there? You'd keep it untouched?"

"Yes, dear. Just ask."

She took another deep breath. She felt dizzied, divorced from reality. The memory of the men on the ice, shadowy in the snow, haunted her. She saw Hal, aching with exhaustion but determined not to quit. If Hal were faced with her choice, she knew what he would do, knew it as surely as she knew her own name. He would choose to keep the bay untouched.

"Well?" said Dagobert.

"Please," she said. Her voice broke slightly, so she tried to say it more clearly. "Please do it. Do it all."

There. She'd said it. Dagobert had won. But so had Hal. The whales would be free, and Bristol Bay would stay as it was.

"Consider it done," said Dagobert, pleasure in his voice. "Now charter a plane and get home as soon as that storm lifts. Leave a note for the Bailey man. Tell him you got bored playing reporter. Tell him your family comes first. Tell him your grandfather has some important social engagements for you. The less said about this little arrangement between you and me, the better. This is family business. And, Jen, it's for your own good, you know. I'm only doing it because I love you."

She listened to the wail of the wind outside. "I know."

She hung up and simply sat, staring at nothing for a long time. Then she got up and mechanically began to pack. She wrote a short note to Hal and slipped it under his door.

"Decided to go home," it said. "I'm tired of playing reporter. I'll think of you, though. Good luck, Jen."

She, who had hoped to make her career through the written word, could think of nothing better to write than those stiff and stilted words. She was too numbed.

She called for a cab, because she would rather wait at the airport than at the base. She knew she would never see Hal or the whales again, Billy or Warren or even grumpy Arnold. She would never see the base or Ultima itself or the endless Arctic plains or the magic of the northern lights.

She was going home, but never again would it seem like home. Never.

CHAPTER ELEVEN

JEN LEFT.

The next day the Soviet ice cutter steamed into the sound exactly as Dagobert had promised. It plowed a channel through the frozen sea, scraped and shuddered its way through the pressure ridge that stood like a wall of ice between the whales and freedom.

The whales swam back to the open sea while people stood on the ice, waving and cheering. Dagobert, who had arranged it all, was hailed as a hero, just as he intended to be.

Every bureau, agency and organization vaguely connected with the rescue also claimed its bit of credit. Few people mentioned Hal's name or those of the Eskimos who had kept the whales alive or led them so near to liberty before the forces of power and privilege took over.

The *Anchorage Daily News* dryly noted that the Eskimos might well have freed the whales, even without the ice cutter, but nobody paid much attention. The story of the Soviets and an elderly American oilman teaming up to help two endangered whales made far better headlines.

As soon as the whales were rescued, Dagobert whisked Jen off to the Mediterranean, for rest and recreation, he said. From Cannes, he pulled off a second publicity coup. He officially announced he was ceasing all attempts to drill in Alaska's Bristol Bay. "I'm an old man," he said in his press release. "It's time I gave something back to this planet, which has given me so much. Never have I been so gratified as by aiding in the rescue of those two whales. From now on, I intend to make the Martinson Corporation a model for the rest of the petroleum industry."

The publicity he got from this announcement, following so soon after the whale rescue, was priceless. Normally such a clever public relations stroke would have filled him with glee. He did not, however, seem gleeful.

Jen was back, and Dagobert had his girl again and all to himself, but she wasn't the same. He complained that she drifted about like a tall, beautiful ghost these days and that she seldom smiled.

She no longer argued with him. She was obedient to a fault. She could tell that Dagobert was growing concerned about her, but she was so unhappy she could not even feign happiness for his benefit, although she still loved him, in spite of everything.

She knew he had planned to dazzle and pamper her back to contentment. She knew, as well, that he had planned their holiday so that it would eclipse every memory of Alaska. He somehow produced a bachelor prince who took her "nightclubbing" in Monte Carlo, and a vacationing president's nephew who took her yachting off the Antibes. The gossip press duly reported these events, but Jen did not enjoy them. All she could think of was a man in a Quonset hut in the Arctic.

She went everywhere Dagobert wished, did whatever he wished, was polite and cordial to whomever he wished, and she was as miserable as it was possible for a woman to be and still keep functioning.

He confronted her one night on the broad balcony of their suite at St. Tropez. She was standing staring out at the moonlight on the sea. She wore an expensive black evening gown for which he'd paid a fortune, thinking, she supposed, that it would make her happy. It hadn't. She simply stood, feeling like an unhappy child dressed up in sophisticate's clothing. She wore her hair pulled back in a chignon, and a breeze played with loose tendrils.

She was lost in her own thoughts, looking past the boats moored in the harbor. Although the night air fluttered warmly around her bare shoulders, she thought of another sea, another coast, another climate, a place where weak or coddled men could not survive.

She heard her grandfather's footsteps and turned, forcing herself to smile. He was practically killing himself to be kind, but she couldn't really appreciate anything he was doing. It was as if she were numb inside.

He came next to her and leaned on the stone wall of the balcony. He looked out at the moon-washed sea. His face was tired. So was his voice. "All right. What do you want?"

She was silent. "I guess I'd like to go home," she said at last.

"Fine." He put an irritable twist on the word. "Then what? Tell me. I'll arrange it. Do you want to go back to work on the paper? Is that it? I'll arrange it with Ferd. I'll arrange whatever you want."

She shook her head and looked back out to sea. "You were right. I wasn't meant to be a reporter. I don't really want just to tell about things. I want to help change them, have some impact. But the truth is, I feel sort of useless. I've been thinking about going back to school."

He looked at her sharply. "School? You want to go to school? Fine. Do anything you want. Just cheer up."

She kept her eyes trained on the sparkling waves. "I want to learn more about the environment. I mean, in Alaska I started thinking about a lot of things I'd never really thought of before. I guess that's what I'd like to do.

Get involved in making the company more concerned about the ecology—the way you promised."

"Fine, fine, fine," he said, "although if I get any more concerned, I'll be broke. What do I care? I'll personally go out and tickle fish under the chin if that's what you want. I'll send chocolate covered sardines to the seals. Fine."

She faced him, and her eyes held his. "I mean it, Dagobert. I want more out of living than just spending your money. I want my life to make a difference in the world, to help make it a better place."

He made an impatient gesture. "Didn't I just say *fine*?"

She nodded. An uneasy silence fell between them. "Another thing," she said, "when we get back—well, don't take this wrong, Dagobert. I need a little time alone. I think I'd like to go down to the lodge at Big Sur for a while. I need to sort things out. I'm sorry—I guess I'm tired. I should go to bed."

She turned to go, but his words halted her. "It's that man, isn't it? You think you're in love with him. Well, you're not. You're young—it's nothing but puppy love, and you'll outgrow it."

She stared at him.

"Besides," Dagobert continued, his ire clearly up, "he doesn't love you. If he did, he'd have come after you. Have you heard a word from him? Well, have you? One word?"

She looked away. "No." It had been four weeks since she had left Alaska. All her mail was being forwarded from the States, and every day she phoned California checking for any calls from Ultima, but there were none. She had heard nothing from Hal. He apparently didn't care about her and wanted nothing more than to forget her, the spoiled rich girl.

"If I thought he was any good for you, I'd tell you to go get him," Dagobert said. "Or I'd get him to come for you. I could do it in a minute if I thought he deserved you. Offer him a position, a stupendous salary—but you have to face it, Jen, he doesn't care."

"He can't be bought," she returned with spirit, the first she'd shown in weeks. "I thought you'd have figured that out by now. You bought *me*, not him. Nobody could buy him."

"I didn't buy you," Dagobert objected. "We had a wager, fair and square. You got yourself in a fix, just as I knew you would, and you needed me to get you out. I saved your blasted whales. I gave up my claim on Bristol Bay. I kept my part of a bargain, that's all. I didn't *buy* you."

Jen studied him. The breeze riffled his white hair and stirred the ruffles of his tuxedo shirt. He looked suddenly old to her, smaller and more frail than he used to. She had no heart to fight with him. Nor had she any right. He was right. He had kept his part of the bargain, and she had agreed to behave if she came home. "Whatever you say."

He shook his head. "Jen, Jen, he's not right for you. He's not your kind. The two of you could never—"

She straightened her back and nodded mechanically. "I know. Let's not talk about it. Good night, Dagobert. Sleep well."

She left him standing alone. "I intend to make you happy, young woman," he called after her. "Whether you like it or not. I'll teach you what's important in this life."

From another part of the hotel, laughter drifted down as if to mock him.

JEN WAS GLAD to be in California again, glad to have time alone in Dagobert's lodge on the coast of Big Sur. He hadn't wanted her to stay alone, but she insisted she could take care of herself and that she would be much better if she simply had a few days to gather her thoughts.

Now the few days had turned into a week. Big Sur, with its green mountains and dizzying cliffs, its Pacific sunsets and crashing surf, was a place where time seemed to have no power. The sea and the stony shore had a sense of the eternal about them, and Jen walked the rough beach every morning and evening, trying to put her life in order.

It was a slightly chill Friday evening with a cool breeze whipping in from the sea. She made her way along the white sand, huddled in her bulky white sweater, her hands in the pockets of her rolled up slacks. The waves beat as steadily as some great, slow heart, and the gulls wheeled and called in the dusky sky. She had taken off her shoes, and the coarse sand was cold beneath her bare feet.

She would have to go home to San Francisco soon, she knew. And she would have to get on with her life. She had to stop grieving for what was lost. But she knew what she had told Dagobert was true. Alaska had changed her, and she would have to take an active part in seeing that the Martinson Corporation became a positive force in environmental concerns. It would have to be transformed. Its metamorphosis would be slow, and it would probably be painful, but it was her duty to see that it was done. And Dagobert, she knew, would allow her the leeway to do it.

The wind rose slightly, and lavender clouds scudded in the darkening sky, heralding night. A pale new moon hung over the sea, and she had a sudden memory of the northern lights, so sharp and vivid a memory that it pained her.

She stopped and stared at the roll of the incoming waves. It wasn't Alaska that had changed her—she knew that. It was Hal. He had made her see the world differently, with more seriousness and concern. He had taught her what integrity meant and what courage was. And he had taught her what desire meant. And loss.

Tears stung her eyes. Dagobert was right. Hal didn't want her or he would have called her, written her, come after her. He had done none of those things. But she could imagine him coming for her, imagine it so clearly that it hurt.

Her vision was blurred, and she could almost see him coming past the huge outcropping of black boulders that stood at the foot of the cliff. He seemed to emerge from the shadow of the rocks, a tall shape moving with intense determination toward her.

The vision was so real that it frightened her, and she wiped her futile tears away. It was terrible, she thought half-angrily, to love the man so much that she was hallucinating about him, because she still seemed to see him, his hands in the pockets of a leather jacket, striding straight toward her.

Her heart missed a beat. She felt cold all over. It was no illusion. *Hal,* Jen thought, *Hal's here.*

Without thinking, she ran toward him, sprinting across the cool, damp sand. Then, suddenly, she slowed, frightened. Her body still felt chilled clear through. She didn't know what it meant, his being there.

She stopped short, just a few paces from him, her breathing uneven again. She stared into a familiar pair of steady blue eyes. Any words she had rehearsed in her imagination fled from her mind.

He stood with his back to the inlet where the waves crashed against the offshore boulders. He wore jeans and a brown leather jacket and no hat. His face was burnished from the northern wind and sun, and he still had something slightly untamed about him, something that it seemed could only be at home in the wild spaces of the world. He looked right, with the tossing sea in the background and the wind in his hair.

She drew her breath in with shock and pleasure. Her heart must have stopped beating, she thought wildly—she could no longer feel it pulsing, and she knew all the blood had left her face. "I—I—" she stuttered. She couldn't finish the sentence. She simply looked at him.

His gaze didn't waver. He took a step toward her, then hesitated. It was as if a dozen invisible barriers separated them—all of the chaos that had run rampant in Ultima, all the misunderstandings, all the power of the Martinson Corporation and MaLaBar Oil, all the machinations of Dagobert.

She wanted to reach out to him. She didn't. He looked wonderful to her, lean and handsome and bronzed by the weather, the power of his gaze as jolting as ever. "Why are you here?"

"For you." His voice was brusque. "I came to thank you."

"Thank me?"

"Keenan says you're responsible for your grandfather pulling out of Bristol Bay. He found out from his grandfather. They've reconciled, you know."

She nodded, still unsure she could trust her knees. "I know." She looked away from him. It was too disturbing to see him again. She hadn't thought it could hurt so much, but it did.

"Jen," he said. "Jennie—look at me. Keenan told me that your grandfather made you come home—that there was some kind of bet. You came home so he'd send the ice cutter. Is it true?"

Still she didn't look at him. She nodded again. "It doesn't matter. It was a stupid bet, but some good came of it, I hope. Has anybody seen any sign of the whales?"

"No. We didn't put radio tags on them. They'd been through enough. I didn't want to chance it."

"Oh." She crossed her arms and stared down into the sand and stones. Her throat was too choked for her to say anything, so she kept silent.

"You should have told me." His voice was harsh. "You were trying to break free the whole time, weren't you? That's why you came to Ultima in the first place. Why didn't you tell me?"

She shrugged and kept staring at the tiles. "It seemed—too personal."

He swore. "Dammit, Jennie, didn't you trust me enough to tell me? Why'd you just walk off like that, without even saying goodbye?"

She raised her eyes to meet his. She lifted her chin. "We'd said goodbye. Remember? You'd told me goodbye already. You didn't want anything to do with me. You said we were too different. That it was like we came from opposite ends of the earth."

"We are different. We do come from opposite ends of the earth." His face was almost rigid with intensity. "But I want to have everything to do with you. Everything."

She regarded him with apprehension. She didn't quite yet believe he was really there. "What?"

"Jenny, there were days when I wanted you more than food or water or air. There were nights when the only thing that kept me going out on that ice was that I loved you so much I'd rather die than fail you—"

Jen blinked hard. "What?" she repeated. "What?"

A muscle worked in his jaw. He glanced out at the sea as if he would be more comfortable fighting its forces than the ones within himself. Then he let his eyes rest on hers again. "I said we're different. And I said that I love you. When you left me, I wanted to walk off into the cold and the dark and never come back. What good would it do to come back? You were gone. I thought you were tired of me. You were a rich girl with everything, and I amused you for a while, but you were bored."

She shook her head, tears rising in her eyes. "I could never be tired of you. Not in a hundred lifetimes."

He closed the distance between them so swiftly that Jen wasn't sure if she'd also moved toward him or not. All she knew was that she was in his arms, held so tightly that nothing could ever wrench her away, and his face was pressed against her hair. She burrowed her face against his chest, trying to get closer still. The leathery scent of his jacket was more wonderful than any perfume.

"Jen...Jennie," he said between his teeth, "I love you. When you left, it was like somebody ripped the sun out of the sky. You told me once that you loved me, and like a fool I didn't want to hear it. Did you mean it? Could you mean it still?"

"Yes," she whispered happily. "Yes." The jacket felt stiff against her face, but more wonderful than silk. She thought she was crying, but didn't know and didn't care.

He held her more tightly still. "I tried to let you go. I couldn't. It doesn't matter that we come from different sides. We'll work it out. We have to. Life's no good without you."

She sighed, running her hands over his sleeves to convince herself he was really there. She turned her face to his. "We'll work it out. I've told my grandfather the company has to change. You made me understand that. You can help me understand how."

"I'll be taking you away from this—" he glanced at the sea and the darkening blue sky.

"Surroundings don't matter." Her voice shook with conviction. "You do. We do. I love you. It's been like dying being away from you."

He shook his head as he drank in her shining face. "I was kind of crazy at first when you left. I wanted to believe you were like a spoiled kid who's tired of a game. I was too tired to think straight. Then your grandfather pulled off a major miracle and things got even crazier than before. I thought you'd used the situation and so had he. Then I heard you were on the Riviera, with the princes and playboys. I was bitter, Jen."

"When I didn't hear from you, I thought you didn't care."

He shook his head impatiently. His voice was taut. "I hadn't been a man who believed in love. Only biological urges and logic. I didn't want to admit what I was feeling, even to myself. But after you were gone, every time I remembered you, something went through me like a knife. And when Keenan told me what had really happened, I thought, what have I lost? What have I let get away from me? What have I done to my life? So I came for you. Will you marry me?"

"When?" she asked. She knew instinctively that she wanted a small wedding, as soon as possible, not the kind of affair she had written about again and again for Ferd's paper. The ceremony was of no importance. Being with Hal and staying with him was what mattered.

"As soon as possible. I've talked to your grandfather, Jen. I went barging into your house in San Francisco looking for you. I told him I wanted to marry you, and that if you'd have me, it didn't matter if he opposed me or not. I told him we could be friends or enemies, it was up to him, but that if you say yes, he'd better get used to me. And not interfere."

She laughed in disbelief. "You told Dagobert not to interfere? That's like telling the tide not to come in and out."

He took her face between his hands, and his expression softened. "Jen, we ended up talking a long time. He told me where to find you. He told me to try to make you happy because he couldn't. He said he knew that by trying to keep you, he'd nearly lost you, and that if he was going to get you back, he'd have to let you go. He said to tell you that he loves you. Enough to set you free. He said he couldn't stand seeing what he'd done to you."

"He said that? Oh, Hal—" She bit her lip to keep it from trembling.

"Hey," he said gently. He took out a white handkerchief and dried her eyes. "Hey, I told you—we'll work everything out. He understands, Jen. There are things more powerful even than he is. Love is one. The kind of love I feel for you is."

He brought his face nearer and kissed her, a long devouring kiss that showed how fierce and single-minded his hunger for her was. "We'll have to go back to Ultima awhile. I hope you don't mind. Billy misses you, too. And Helena wants to meet you. Then we can come back to California if you want. I've got a job offer here. And one in the Caribbean."

"I'd love to go back to Ultima," she said. "I want to see the lights playing in the sky. I want to look at the frozen sea. I want to visit the place where Goofus and Doofus were, and where you worked so hard."

"We," he corrected and kissed her again. "*We* worked so hard. And we did it. Together. Somehow, in some crazy way, everything came together, and the world may have gotten its happy ending. You made it happen, from beginning to end. But you almost killed me when you left."

"Then I'll never leave again."

He smiled. "The sun's down for the winter in Ultima. You're going to have a wedding night two months long."

She smiled back. "It's cold there, too. You'll have to keep me warm."

"I intend to keep you warm for the rest of your life. Warm and needed and loved." Once more he tasted her lips.

Jen sighed happily and wound her arms around his neck.

FAR OUT IN THE SEA beyond Big Sur, two shapes rose under the starlight. Triangles of spray shimmered in the air. Two faces, scarred with white from healed cuts and frostbite, felt the warm air. Keeping close together, the two animals breathed freely, in giant, sighing gasps. Then they plunged and swam on, disappearing toward the mating grounds.

And on shore Hal kissed Jen again, and she kissed him back.

PASSPORT TO ROMANCE VACATION SWEEPSTAKES

OFFICIAL RULES

SWEEPSTAKES RULES AND REGULATIONS. NO PURCHASE NECESSARY.

HOW TO ENTER:

1. To enter, complete this official entry form and return with your invoice in the envelope provided, or print your name, address, telephone number and age on a plain piece of paper and mail to: Passport to Romance, P.O. Box #1397, Buffalo, N.Y. 14269-1397. No mechanically reproduced entries accepted.
2. All entries must be received by the Contest Closing Date, midnight, December 31, 1990 to be eligible.
3. Prizes: There will be ten (10) Grand Prizes awarded, each consisting of a choice of a trip for two people to: i) London, England (approximate retail value $5,050 U.S.); ii) England, Wales and Scotland (approximate retail value $6,400 U.S.); iii) Caribbean Cruise (approximate retail value $7,300 U.S.); iv) Hawaii (approximate retail value $ 9,550 U.S.); v) Greek Island Cruise in the Mediterranean (approximate retail value $12,250 U.S.); vi) France (approximate retail value $7,300 U.S.).
4. Any winner may choose to receive any trip or a cash alternative prize of $5,000.00 U.S in lieu of the trip.
5. Odds of winning depend on number of entries received.
6. A random draw will be made by Nielsen Promotion Services, an independent judging organization on January 29, 1991, in Buffalo, N.Y., at 11:30 a.m. from all eligible entries received on or before the Contest Closing Date. Any Canadian entrants who are selected must correctly answer a time-limited, mathematical skill-testing question in order to win. Quebec residents may submit any litigation respecting the conduct and awarding of a prize in this contest to the Régie des loteries et courses du Quebec.
7. Full contest rules may be obtained by sending a stamped, self-addressed envelope to: "Passport to Romance Rules Request", P.O. Box 9998, Saint John, New Brunswick, E2L 4N4.
8. Payment of taxes other than air and hotel taxes is the sole responsibility of the winner.
9. Void where prohibited by law.

PASSPORT TO ROMANCE VACATION SWEEPSTAKES

OFFICIAL RULES

SWEEPSTAKES RULES AND REGULATIONS. NO PURCHASE NECESSARY.

HOW TO ENTER:

1. To enter, complete this official entry form and return with your invoice in the envelope provided, or print your name, address, telephone number and age on a plain piece of paper and mail to: Passport to Romance, P.O. Box #1397, Buffalo, N.Y. 14269-1397. No mechanically reproduced entries accepted.
2. All entries must be received by the Contest Closing Date, midnight, December 31, 1990 to be eligible.
3. Prizes: There will be ten (10) Grand Prizes awarded, each consisting of a choice of a trip for two people to: i) London, England (approximate retail value $5,050 U.S.); ii) England, Wales and Scotland (approximate retail value $6,400 U.S.); iii) Caribbean Cruise (approximate retail value $7,300 U.S.); iv) Hawaii (approximate retail value $ 9,550 U.S.); v) Greek Island Cruise in the Mediterranean (approximate retail value $12,250 U.S.); vi) France (approximate retail value $7,300 U.S.).
4. Any winner may choose to receive any trip or a cash alternative prize of $5,000.00 U.S. in lieu of the trip.
5. Odds of winning depend on number of entries received.
6. A random draw will be made by Nielsen Promotion Services, an independent judging organization on January 29, 1991, in Buffalo, N.Y., at 11:30 a.m. from all eligible entries received on or before the Contest Closing Date. Any Canadian entrants who are selected must correctly answer a time-limited, mathematical skill-testing question in order to win. Quebec residents may submit any litigation respecting the conduct and awarding of a prize in this contest to the Régie des loteries et courses du Quebec.
7. Full contest rules may be obtained by sending a stamped, self-addressed envelope to: "Passport to Romance Rules Request", P.O. Box 9998, Saint John, New Brunswick, E2L 4N4.
8. Payment of taxes other than air and hotel taxes is the sole responsibility of the winner.
9. Void where prohibited by law.

 RLS-DIR

VACATION SWEEPSTAKES

MONTH 2 ENTRY

Official Entry Form

Yes, enter me in the drawing for one of ten Vacations-for-Two! If I'm a winner, I'll get my choice of any of the six different destinations being offered — and I won't have to decide until after I'm notified!

Return entries with invoice in envelope provided along with Daily Travel Allowance Voucher. Each book in your shipment has two entry forms — and the more you enter, the better your chance of winning!

Name ______________________________

Address ______________________________ Apt.

City ______________ State/Prov. ______________ Zip/Postal Code

Daytime phone number ______________________________
Area Code

☐ I am enclosing a Daily Travel Allowance Voucher in the amount of $__________ Write in amount revealed beneath scratch-off

- -

PASSPORT
WIN
1 of 10 Vacations
SEE INSIDE
TO ROMANCE

VACATION SWEEPSTAKES

MONTH 2 ENTRY

Official Entry Form

Yes, enter me in the drawing for one of ten Vacations-for-Two! If I'm a winner, I'll get my choice of any of the six different destinations being offered — and I won't have to decide until after I'm notified!

Return entries with invoice in envelope provided along with Daily Travel Allowance Voucher. Each book in your shipment has two entry forms — and the more you enter, the better your chance of winning!

Name ______________________________

Address ______________________________ Apt.

City ______________ State/Prov. ______________ Zip/Postal Code

Daytime phone number ______________________________
Area Code

☐ I am enclosing a Daily Travel Allowance Voucher in the amount of $__________ Write in amount revealed beneath scratch-off

CPS-TWO